D1266648

THE CARDIFF TEAM

Also by Guy Davenport

FICTION

Tatlin!
Da Vinci's Bicycle
Eclogues
Trois Caprices
Apples and Pears
The Bicycle Rider
The Jules Verne Steam Balloon
The Drummer of the Eleventh North Devonshire Fusiliers
A Table of Green Fields

ESSAYS

The Geography of the Imagination
Every Force Evolves a Form
A Balthus Notebook

POETRY

Flowers and Leaves
Thasos and Ohio

TRANSLATIONS

7 Greeks
The Logia of Yeshua (with Benjamin Urrutia)

Guy Davenport

THE CARDIFF TEAM

Ten Stories

A NEW DIRECTIONS BOOK

ACKNOWLEDGMENTS

These stories are published here for the first time, except for "Dinner at the Bank of England," which appeared in *The Paris Review,* "The Meadow Lark," which was issued as a book called *The Lark* by Barry Magid at his Dim Gray Bar Press, and some excerpts from "The Cardiff Team," which ran in *Conjunctions.* To Dr. Magid, Bradford Morrow, and the editors of *The Paris Review,* the author is grateful for permission to reprint.

Manufactured in the United States of America
New Directions Books are printed on acid-free paper
First published clothbound in 1996
Published simultaneously in Canada by Penguin Books Canada Limited

Library of Congress Cataloging-in-Publication Data

Davenport, Guy.
The Cardiff team : ten stories / Guy Davenport.
p. cm.
ISBN 0-8112-1335-8
I. Title
PS3554.A86C37 1996
813'.54-dc20 96-24208
CIP

New Directions Books are published for James Laughlin
by New Directions Publishing Corporation,
80 Eighth Avenue, New York 10011

TABLE OF CONTENTS

THE CARDIFF TEAM

The Messengers

His cabin at the Jungborn Spa in the Harz Mountains had large windows without curtains or shutters and a glass door so that sunlight fell in on all fours after its abrupt journey through space, home at last. Some pipe-smoking architect in knickerbockers who had seen English country cottages in *The Studio* had fused a *Mon Repos* with *Jugendstil* in its rectilinear and functional mode and come up with this many-windowed shoe box, perhaps with the help of an elf and a Marxist agronomist. He had never before had a house all to himself.

A naked idealist was already pushing a pamphlet under the door. An army of geese was making its way into the meadow.

His visions of *Naturheilkunde* were largely from *Náš Skautík,* the sun-gilded youth in which, awash with air and light, springing from rock to rock across streams, hatcheting saplings and roping them into structures with the genius of beavers, made him feel like Ivan Ilych envying rude health.

But the pamphleteer, whom he could see continuing along the dirt road, bowlegged, was bald and round-shouldered, and an elephant's tail would have fitted right in on his behind.

Would a household god set up shop in this cabin? Wouldn't its reek of sawn pine and shellac and the chemical aroma of the linoleum be uncongenial to a *lar* who for thousands of years was used to rising dough, peasants' stockings, and wine?

Outside, July. He could see the vast roof of the *pensione* over the trees. The cabins were set romantically along the leafy roads, or tucked into dells and glades.

The pamphlet was about vegetarianism and the diffusion of Mind throughout Nature. Just so.

Now for patience. It was impatience that got us thrown out of the Garden, and impatience keeps us from returning. Air and light and peace of soul were why he was here. Carrot juice and lectures. Presumably his effects were safe in his suitcase on the folding trestle at the foot of the bed. He laid out his toothbrush and comb beside the pitcher and basin. The household god, named Mildew or Jug Ears, must have noted him by this time, peeping from around the chamber pot or from inside the lamp. There was no key to the cabin.

Once, when there was a choice of being kings or messengers, we, being children, chose to be messengers, arms and legs flying as we romped from castle to castle. We got the messages wrong as like as not, or forgot them, or fell asleep in the forest while kings died of anxiety.

Bathing drawers. He would go out to the meadow, where he could see a man reading two books at once, in bathing drawers. Everybody else that he could see was nude.

And there, as he drew them on, watching him with an innocent smile, was the household god, its cap respectfully in its hands.

—My name is Beeswax, it said. I am going to sleep in your shoe. What is your name?

—My name? Why, it's Amschel. I mean, Franz. By the world I am Franz Kafka.

—A *kavka* is a jackdaw.

—A grackle. *Graculus,* in Latin a blackbird.

—Yes.

Max was used to conversations between chairs in letters and would not challenge a household god in a cabin at a nudist health spa.

—Max Brod, my best friend, will like hearing about you. He and I have been travelling together. We visited Goethe's house. I dreamed that night of a rabbit in a Sicilian garden. I am here to breathe all the fresh air I can and to bathe in sunlight. So I'm going out now, to the meadow.

—Yes. I will look at your things. If you should chance upon a garden, I would like a turnip. The buttons on your shoes are particularly interesting.

From the people he met along the road he got sweet smiles or analytical stares. Walking and dawdling was apparently part of the therapy. Some were as white as he, some pink, some brown. On a path into the meadow a gentleman wearing only a pince-nez and a knotted handkerchief on his bald head referred to its narrowness as *these Dardanelles.* He heard talk of Steiner and rhythmic awakenings.

His bathing drawers were a mistake. The logic of nudism was to be nude, but nude and naked were different conditions. Michelangelo's David was nude and the lean scouts in *Náš Skautík* were nude in or out of their short khaki pants, but the old fart over there with wings of hair out from his ears and pregnant with a volley ball, with spindle legs and wrinkled knees, is naked.

They were twins, the boys who crossed the path in front of him, or cousins or brothers very close in age, two young Swedes who, God knows, may be Swedenborgians, more likely Lutherans, perhaps Baptists of some sect with pure morals, sonorous hymns sung to fiddles and concertinas, and sermons three hours long in a wooden church through the windows of which you could see birches and cedars and snow. But now they were Castor and Pollux in an Austrian meadow.

Later, when he was going to the lodge to mail his letter to Max, they crossed his way again, naked as ancient Greeks at Elis, healthy as dogs, honey brown from the sun, their hair the color of meal, their large eyes blue.

Next day, the pink evangelist lying in the meadow reading two bibles at once bade Kafka good day and asked his opinion of prophecy.

His books were under an umbrella stuck in the meadow. He himself, pink as coral, was undergoing heliotherapy on a Navajo blanket.

—Here in First Samuel, he said. A company of prophets coming down with a psaltery, a pipe, and a harp, an event itself prophesied.

—My opinion would be an ignorant one.

The two Swedish boys, Jonathan and David, came side by side from the path in the pine wood. They walked like people holding hands, shoulder to shoulder, in step.

A company of prophets from the bare rock of a high place came down, dancing stately forward, with a raised knee and a straight knee, with a gliding step and a stomp, in time to a tabret, exalted by the chime of a harp and the trill of a flute, prophesying. *Is Saul also among the prophets?*

—Everyone, Kafka smiled, seems to have a message for me, as if I'd fallen among prophets.

—A word to the wise, said the evangelist. The Lord knows his own.

The noises outside his cabin at night were probably messages, but not for him: field mice passing on to field mice the advance of the summer according to the stars and the latest news of the Balkan wars. He had gone out in the deep of night, to lean wholly naked against his door, for the liberty of it. He had never had a door, nor the freedom to stand like Adam in moonlight.

But moonlight, Dr. Schlaf said in his lecture, is bad for you, along with wearing modern clothes, eating fruit, and thinking pessimistically. He had been an officer, Dr. Schlaf, in what army he did not specify, and had the refined manners of an insane aristocrat, speaking delicately with his fingertips together, with moist eyes open wide. He had published several works, which Kafka as an educated man would find interesting.

—You will know how to weigh my words and draw your own conclusions.

The day began with calisthenics in a group, with a phonograph playing marches to keep time to. The exercises were from Etienne-Jules Marey's manual for the French army, as modified by Swedish gymnasts for civilian health and beauty.

Adolf Just, the director of the Jungborn Spa for Naturtherapie had invented the Nudist Crawl whereby they went on all fours in a wide circle. The Swedish boys moved like elegant greyhounds.

Here in the countryside, ankle-deep in nameless meadow flowers, metaphysics and jurisprudence were as outcast as Adam and Eve from their paradise in Eden. God did not destroy that garden. He put us out of it. It is still where it was, going to seed for lack of care, or flourishing under divine husbandry. Or waiting in the orange groves of Palestine for agronomists like Ottla.

Max found in a book that the American follower of Jakob Boehme Ralph Waldo Emerson had gone blind and lame in some theological yeshiva of the Protestants and sought to restore his health by becoming a common farm laborer, weeding turnips and hoeing rows of maize. On this farm he met a fellow worker named Tarbox, of the Methodist sect. Theology was their constant topic. Herr Emerson was wondering one day if indeed God ever pays the least attention to our prayers.

—Yes He does, said Farmer Tarbox, and our trouble is that He answers them all.

It was a strategy of the sacred to appear in disguise, like Tobias's angel, a prosperous kinsman. The most biblical thing they were doing at the spa was working on the model farm like Pastor Emerson. They pitched hay onto a wagon behind the angels with scythes. On ladders out of Flemish painting they picked cherries. The first evening after pitching hay he read the Book of Ruth. There was a bible in every cabin.

To read in an Austrian meadow texts written in the desert was a kind of miracle. The thirtieth year after Hilkiah the priest found the book of the law in the house of the sanctuary, at midnight, after the setting of the moon, in the days of Josiah the king.

—To care for the body, the evangelist said, wiping his brow with a blue handkerchief, to live cleanly here in this pure air, soaking in the vital influences of the sun, is to move toward an awakening of the soul from doubt and sloth. Here, take this pamphlet, *The Prodigal Son,* and this one, *Bought, or No Longer Mine: For Unbelieving Believers.*

Kafka mentioned, quietly, the inner light, his conscience.

—And this one, *Why Can't the Educated Man Believe in the Bible?*

The Swedish godlings strolled up, stopping at a safe distance, to listen. Their long foreskins puckered at the tip. Their pubic hair was a tawny orange. Their rumps were dimpled just back of the hip, as if to indicate that their long legs were well socketed. They were as comely, slender, and graceful as deer. They were like Asahel in Samuel, as swift of foot as the wild gazelle. Like the young David they were ruddy and had beautiful eyes.

—There is no prospect of grace for me, Kafka said.

He could not match the evangelist's staring sincerity, and lowered his eyes.

A thin old man with white hair and a red nose joined them, offering a remark from time to time, perhaps in Chaldean.

—Are you a Mormon? the evangelist asked. A Theosophist? But as a lawyer from Prague you are a Darwinian, aren't you?

Again Kafka pleaded the inviolable inwardness of the heart.

—Is Darwin among the prophets?

The old man, after coughing and wiping his lips, made another remark in Chaldean.

Castor and Pollux smiled as sweetly as angels.

He dreamed that his fellow nudists all annihilated each other. It was a battle of the naked against the naked, as in Mantegna. They kicked and drove swift blows with their fists. It started when they formed into two groups, joking and then taunting. A stalwart fellow took command of his group and shouted at the other.

—Lustron and Kastron!

—Ach! Lustron and Kastron?

—Exactly!

And then the brawl began, like fanatics in Goya. When it was over, there was nothing of them left. The vast meadow was empty.

Kafka woke, wondering.

Could the household god see his dreams? What would Dr. Freud say? What in the world do *lustron* and *kastron* mean?

The habit he had fallen into of seeing the well-built Swedish boys as Castor and Pollux, disregarding that their minds were a vegetation of ignorance, superstition, folklore, archaic fears, provincial opinions, and Lutheran piety, and that any conversation he might have with them would be about automobiles and Jesus, had something to do with the dream.

Latin endings rather than Greek would make the words into *castrum,* a castle, and *lustrum,* a cleansing. Pollux, *pollutum,* a defiling. Clean and filthy: antitheses. When antithetical particles in the atomic theory collide, they annihilate each other.

Castor and Pollux could not exist simultaneously. One could live only when the other was dead, a swap made by loving brothers.

In the botanical garden at Jena by the elephant ear, in his charcoal coat with the blue collar, Friedrich Schlegel said that a fragment should be complete in itself, like a porcupine.

To Castor and Pollux, next they bowed to him in passing, and while they were smiling in their innocent nudity, *I am a lawyer,* he might remark, *and I have a sister who is an agronomist.* This would probably sound like *I am a judge but I have a little brother who spins tops.*

And Castor would inquire of Pollux, *What are an agronomist?* The sun-browned fingers of a classical hand would scratch around in hair the color of meal. Blue eyes would puzzle themselves closed.

—She makes trees grow. She plans to emigrate to Palestine and grow oranges and apricots. Sinai apples. Golden green oranges.

Pollux would look at Castor, Castor at Pollux.

Opposites do not cooperate. They annihilate each other.

It was next day, while talking with Herr Guido von Gillshausen, the retired captain who writes poetry and music, that he learned that the beautiful Swedish boys were named Jeremias and Barnabas. They had bowed as they passed, and the captain had spoken to them by name. Fine specimens, were they not?

In the evening Kafka was invited to a rifle meet by Dr. Schlaf and a Berlin hairdresser. The broad plain sloping up to the Bugberg was bordered by very old lindens and cut across by a railroad. The shooting was from a platform. Peasants near the targets kept score in a ledger. While the shooting cracked, fifers with women's handkerchiefs down their backs played sprightly airs. They wore medievil smocks. The rifles were ancient muzzle-loaders.

A band arrived, playing a colorful march, and regimental banners from the time of Napoleon were paraded past, with excited applause from both the villagers and the patients at the spa. Then a drum-and-fife corps caused even greater excitement. Meanwhile, the firing went on, with shouts of bull's-eyes. In the awfullest bombardments in the American Civil War the bands had continued to play waltzes and polkas.

When the shooting was over, they all marched away to the band, at the dying of the day under banked storm clouds, the Champion Shot at the head of the procession in a top hat and with a scarlet sash wound around his frock coat.

Jeremias and Barnabas had not come to the rifle meet. Perhaps they were determined to remain mother-naked for their stay at the spa. At home in Sweden did they wear large-sleeved pleated shirts and tight knee-pants, flat Protestant black hats and tasseled hobnail shoes?

Had they a language other than Swedish? The spa was the lower slopes of the Tower of Babel. Herr Just did his best with nouns and their equivalents, along with a wild irresponsibility of verbs. A family all with crossed eyes could not understand *dinner* or *supper* or *evening meal* but, *ja ja,* they wanted something to eat. A woman in a large straw hat told him all about Prague, where she had never been. It was discovered that he, *the man in the bathing trunks,* bought strawberry sodas for girls, from serious six-year-olds to giggling and brazen sixteen-year-olds, none of whom had either conversation or gratitude.

One evening his matches could not be found when he returned to his cabin. He borrowed a match from the cabin down the lane and by its light looked under his table. He found his water glass there. The lamp was under the bed, and when he'd lit it he saw that his chamber pot was on a ledge over the closet door, his matches were on the windowsill, his sandals were tucked behind the mirror. His inkwell and wet washcloth were under the blanket on the bed. Austrian humor.

The household god was nowhere to be seen.

—Beeswax? he called. Come out, the pranksters are gone.

He put the lamp on the bedside table and opened his *Education sentimentale.* If he were at home his mother would say he was simultaneously ruining his eyes and wasting oil.

His cabin by lamplight was as congenial and private a place as he had ever longed for.

Light in a copse of small trees, softened by leaves, could not be suspected of having come from the raging furnace of the sun. And why is the hospitality of the one inhabited planet so consistently inadequate? The terror of God and his angels has grown remote over the years, but like the sun it is still there, raging.

At Goethe's house with Max he had remembered that when Eckermann paid his first visit he was thoroughly and silently inspected inside the door by the poet's pretty grandsons Walter and Wolfgang. Then they flew clattering and tumbling to tell Grossvater that a stranger had come in from the street. Messengers.

The white geese by the pond were the German soul.

The angels who came to Sodom were two. The message they brought is unrecorded. They only said that they preferred to spend the night in the street. They were antithetical beings annihilating a city. Like long-legged Jeremias and Barnabas they had perhaps forgotten the message they had so carefully memorized, or lost it on the way, having set out like children, elbows high and hair flopping in their eyes, feet flying, and come to a meadow where it would be jolly to pick flowers, or a river to skip pebbles on.

How long had the book of the law been lost when Hilkiah the priest found it in the house of the sanctuary, at midnight, after the setting of the moon, in the days of Josiah the king?

—Beeswax, where are you?

How peaceful, the night. He would learn next day, from sly comments he was meant to overhear, that it was the girls for whom he bought strawberry sodas who disarranged his cabin.

—I am here, Beeswax said, in your shoe.

—What are the crickets saying?

—Some are saying *yes* and some are saying *no*. Their language has only those two words.

From empty castle to empty castle the messengers are flying, backtracking to find a lost shoe, stopping to pick berries, asking cows and sparrows the way from here to there, happy and proud in their importance.

Dinner at the Bank of England

—Bank of England, guvnor? Bank of England'll be closed this time of day.

Jermyn Street, gaslit and foggy on this rainy evening in 1901, pleased Mr Santayana in its resemblance to a John Atkinson Grimshaw, correct and gratifyingly English, the redbrick church across from his boarding house at No. 87 serenely *there,* like all of St. James, on civilization's firmest rock.

—Nevertheless, the Bank of England.

—Climb in, then, the cabman said. Slipped his keeper, he said to his horse. Threadneedle Street, old girl, and then what?

Quadrupedente sonitu they clopped through the rain until, with a knowing sigh, the cabman reined up at the Bank of England. Mr Santayana, having emerged brolly first, popping it open, paid the driver, tipping him with American generosity.

—I'll wait, guvnor. You'll never get in, you know.

But a bobby had already come forward, saluting.

—This way, sir.

—I'll be buggered, the cabman said.

The inner court, where light from open doors reflected from puddles, polished brass, and sabres, was full of guards in scarlet coats with white belts, a livelier and more colorful *Night Watch* by a more Hellenistic Rembrandt.

The room where he had been invited to dinner by Captain Geoffrey Stewart was Dickensian, with a congenial coal fire in the grate under a walnut mantelpiece.

Captain Stewart, as fresh and youthful as he had been when they met the year before in Boston, was out of his scarlet coat, which hung by its shoulders on the back of a chair in which sat his bearskin helmet. A stately and superbly British butler took Santayana's brolly, derby, and coat with the hint of an indulgent, approving smile. Whether he had been told that the guest was a professor from Harvard or whether he read his clothes, shoes, and face as gentry of some species, he clearly accepted him as a gentleman proper enough to dine with his captain.

—You mean Victorian fug when you say *Dickensian,* the captain laughed. I have to do an inspection round at eleven, but as I believe I said, you're a lawful guest until then. The bylaws of the Bank of England allow the captain of the guard to have one guest, male. The fare is thought to be suitable for soldiers, and here's Horrocks with the soup, mock turtle, and boiled halibut with egg sauce will be along, mutton, gooseberry tart with cream, and anchovies on toast, to be washed down with these cold bottles, for you I'm afraid, I've been taken off wine. Not, I imagine, your idea of a meal. Horrocks knows it's just right for his young gentlemen in scarlet.

—Philosophers, Santayana said, eat what's put before them.

—High table at Harvard will be amused. I'm awfully pleased you could come.

A handsome young barbarian out of Kipling, the captain's manners were derived from a nanny and from a public school and modified by an officer's mess. The British are charming among equals and superiors, fair to underlings, and pleasantly artificial to all except family and closest friends.

—But you can't, you know, saddle yourself with being a foreigner. I gather your family is Spanish but that you are a colonial, growing up in Boston and all that. Most colonials are more English than the English. You see that in Canadians. Your George Washington Irving, we were told at school, is as pukka British as any of our authors. Longfellow also. Same language, I mean to say.

—My native tongue is Spanish.

—Not a trace of accent. Of course you don't *look* English, I mean American, but then you can't go by that, can you? Most of the

Danes I've seen look more English than we do, when they don't look like Scots. You look South American. It's the moustache and the small bones, what? I know a Spanish naval officer with absolutely the frame of a girl. Probably cut my throat if I were to say so, devilish touchy, your Spaniard. Doesn't Shakespeare say so somewhere?

—I'm various kinds of hybrid. Bostonians are a breed apart in the United States. I can lay claim to being an aristocrat, but only through intermarriages. As a Catholic I'm an outcast, and as a Catholic atheist I am a kind of unique pariah.

—That's jolly!

—I am, I think, the only materialist alive. But a Platonic materialist.

—I haven't a clue what that could mean. Sounds a bit mad.

—Doubtless it is. This wine is excellent.

—No offence, my dear fellow, you understand? Our fire needs a lump or two of coal. Horrocks!

—The unexamined life is eminently worth living, were anyone so fortunate. It would be the life of an animal, brave and alert, with instincts instead of opinions and decisions, loyalty to mate and cubs, to the pack. It might, for all we know, be a life of richest interest and happiness. Dogs dream. The quickened spirit of the eagle circling in high cold air is beyond our imagination. The placidity of cattle shames the Stoic, and what critic has the acumen of a cat? We have used the majesty of the lion as a symbol of royalty, the wide-eyed stare of owls for wisdom, the mild beauty of the dove for the spirit of God.

—You talk like a book, what? One second, here's somebody coming. Sorry to interrupt.

Horrocks opened the door to admit a seven-foot corporal, who saluted and stamped his feet.

—Sir, Collins's taken ill, sir. Come all over queasy like, sir, and shivering something pitiful, sir.

Captain Stewart stood, found a note case in his jacket on the back of a chair, and ordered the corporal to pop Collins into a cab and take him to the dispensary.

—Here's a quid. Bring back a supernumerary. Watkins will sub for you.
—Sir, good as done, sir.
—Thank you, corporal.

And to Santayana, picking a walnut from the bowl and cracking it expertly:
—Hate chits. Rather pay from my own pocket than fill up a form. I suppose I have an education. Latin and Greek are cheerful little games, if you have the brains for them, and most boys do. Batty generals in Thucydides, Caesar in Gaul throwing up palisades and trenching fosses. Never figured out Horace at all.
—There are more books in the British Museum about Horace than any other writer.
—My God!
—Civilization is diverse. You can omit Horace without serious diminishment. I look on the world as a place we have made more or less hospitable, and at some few moments magnificent. When would you have liked to live, had you the choice, and where?
—Lord knows. Do drink up. Horrocks will think you don't appreciate the Bank of England's port. Eighteenth century? On the Plains of Abraham. The drums, the pipers, the Union Jack in the morning light. Wolfe reciting Gray's *Elegy* before the attack, to calm his nerves. Wouldn't have thought that there was a nerve in his body. Absolute surprise to the French, as if the army had appeared from nowhere. I would have liked to have been there.
—That plangent name, both biblical and Shakespearean, the Plains of Abraham. It was simply Farmer Abraham's cow pasture.
—Is it, now? Well, Bannockburn's a trout stream and Hastings a quiet village.
—And Lepanto the empty sea.

Horrocks permitted himself a brightened eye and sly smile. He was serving quality, after all.
—English mustard is one of the delights of your pleasant country. My friends the Russells would be appalled to know that one

of my early discoveries here was cold meat pie with mustard and beer. I like to think that Chaucer and Ben Jonson wrote with them at their elbow.

—There's a half-batty Colonel Herbert-Kenny, in Madras I believe, who writes cookbooks under the name Wyvern. These address themselves to supplying a British mess with local vegetables, condiments, and meat. Simplicity is his word. All the world's problems come from a lack of simplicity in anything you might think of, food, dress, manners. The bee in his bonnet is that food is character and that to eat Indian is to whore after strange gods. That's scripture, isn't it?

—He's right. Spinoza and Epicurus were Spartan eaters.

—I thought Epicurus was a gourmet, or gourmand, banquets and puking?

—He has that reputation, a traditional misunderstanding. He ate simply. He did insist on exquisite taste, but the fare was basic and elementary.

—Herbert-Kenny must have read his books.

—Cheese and bread, olives and cold water. He and Thoreau would have got along.

—Not familiar with this Thoreau, a Frenchman?

—A New Englander, hermit and mystic. Americans run to originality.

—Examined his soul, did he? I heard a lot of that in America.

Horrocks poked up the fire, removed plates, replenished Santayana's glass, silently, almost invisibly.

The dormitory and the barracks had shaped his world. He was probably far more ignorant of sensual skills than an Italian ten-year-old, a virgin who would be awkward with his county wife, and would become a domestic tyrant and brute, but a good father to daughters and just but not affectionate one to sons.

Their friendship was a sweet mystery. The British explain nothing, and do not like to have things explained. The captain had doubtless told his friends that he'd met this American who was dashedly friendly when he was in Boston, had even given him a book about Harvard College, where he was a professor wallah. Followed sports, the kind of rugger they call football in America. Keen on wrestling and track. Speaks real French and German to waiters, and once remarked, as a curiosity, that he always dreams in Spanish. Says we English are the Romans of our time, but Romans crossbred with Protestantism and an inch from being fanatics except that good Roman horse sense, which we take from the classics, and a native decency and love of animals keep us from being Germans. Talks like a book, but no airs about him at all.

—I like this room, Santayana said. It is England. The butler, fireplace, and mantel out of Cruikshank, the walnut chairs, the sporting prints, the polished brass candlesticks. You yourself, if a foreigner who reads may make the observation, are someone to be encountered in Thackeray or Kipling.

—Oh I say! That's altogether too fanciful. No butlers in America?

—Only Irish girls who drop the soup.

—Back to your being a materialist, Captain Stewart said. I'm interested.

—Your Samuel Butler was a materialist, the Englishman of Englishmen in our time. He was a sane Voltaire who was wholly disillusioned intellectually while being in bondage to his comfort and his heart, a character Dickens might have invented if he hadn't his readers to consider. The nonconformist is an English type, a paradox the English themselves fail to appreciate, for they have long forgotten that exceptions might be a threat to the community. An American Butler, even if he sounded like Emerson, would find himself too often in hot water.

—Don't know this Butler. Is *materialist* a technical term?

—The world is evident. Begin there.

The captain laughed.

—The substantiality and even the presence of the world have been called into doubt by serious minds, by Hindus, by Chinese poets, by Bishop Berkeley and German idealists.

—Extraordinary! Hindus! I daresay. And your being a materialist is your firm belief that the world is, as you put it, evident? Does all this have anything to do with anything?

Santayana laughed.

—No. What interests me is that all thought and therefore all action stands on a quicksand of tacit assumptions. What we believe is what we are and what we expect of others, and of fate.

—Here's my corporal again.

—Sir, Collins is taken care of, sir.

—Carry on, corporal.

—Sir! Yes sir!

—Spirit lives in matter, which gives rise to it. We are integral with matter. We eat, we breathe, we generate, we ache. Existence is painful.

—Do try the walnuts. They're excellent. Do you think we live in good times or bad? I mean, do you want us all to be materialists?

—I am content to let every man and woman be themselves. I am not them. When man is at last defeated and his mind bound with ungiving chains, it will be through a cooperation of science and what now passes for liberalism. That is, through his intellect and his concept of the good, just, and useful life. This is, of course, a cruel paradox, but it is real and inevitable. Science is interested only in cause and effect, in naked demonstrable truth. It will eventually tell us that consciousness is chemical and the self a congeries of responses to stimuli. Liberalism is on a course of analyzing culture into a system of political allegiances which can be explained by science, and controlled by sanctions, all with the best of intentions. All of life's surprises will be prevented, all spontaneity strangled by proscriptions, all variety canceled. White light conceals all its colors, which appear only through refractions, that is, through irregularity and pervasive differences. Liberalism in its triumphant maturity will be its opposite, an opaque tyranny and a repression through benevolence which no tyrant however violent has ever achieved.

—Here here! You're talking for effect, as at the Union.

—There is no fanaticism like sweet reason. You are as yet free, being wonderfully young, and having the advantage of the liberty of the army.
—Liberty, you say?
—The most freedom anyone can enjoy is in constraint that looks the other way from time to time. You know that from childhood and from school.
—The army is school right on. And one does and doesn't long to be out. I can't see myself as a major in India, parboiled by the climate and becoming more conservative and apoplectic by the hour.
—Youth does not have as much of childhood in it as early maturity has youth. There is an abrupt demarcation between child and adolescent, a true metamorphosis.
—Something like, yes.
—The English fireside is as congenial an institution as your culture has to offer. We Americans find your bedrooms arctic and your rain a trial, but the saloon of the King's Arms in Oxford, after freezing in the Bodleian or walking in the meadows, is my idea of comfort. As is this room, as well. And as a philosopher who speaks his mind, I delight in your receiving and feeding me in your picturesque undress, those terribly uncomfortable-looking galluses, do you call them? over your plain Spartan undyed shirt. I might be the guest of a young Viking in his house clothes.
—You should hear the major on the subject of gravy on a tunic. And you decline to convert me to materialism. What, then, to believe? Horrocks and I ought to have something to benefit us from a Harvard professor's coming to dine.
—We seem to need belief, don't we? Skepticism is more than likely unintelligent. It is certainly uncomfortable and lonely. Well, let's see. Believe that everything, including spirit and mind, is composed of earth, air, fire, and water.
—That is probably what I have always believed. But, look here, my dear fellow, it's coming up eleven, when I must be on parade

in the dead of night, with drums and fifes. All civilians must be home in their beds. Look, Horrocks will give you to the corporal, who will give you to the bobby outside, and you're on your own. This has been awfully jolly.

—It has, indeed, said Santayana, shaking hands.

—Good night, sir, Horrocks offered.

—Good night, and thank you, Santayana said, tending him a shilling.

The rain had let up. He would walk to Jermyn Street, keeping the image of Captain Stewart in his martial undress lively in his imagination, as Socrates must have mused on Lysis's perfect body, or on Alcibiades whose face Plutarch wrote was the handsomest in all of Greece. The world is a spectacle, and a gift.

The perfect body is itself the soul.

If he was a guest at the Bank of England, he was equally a guest at his boarding house on Jermyn Street, the world his host. Emerson said that the joy of an occasion was in the beholder not in the occasion. He is wrong. Geoffrey Stewart is real, his beauty real, his spirit real. I have not imagined him, or his fireside, or his butler, or his wide shoulders or the tuft of ginger hair showing where the top button was left unbuttoned on his clean Spartan undervest.

Suppose that in a Spanish town I came upon an apparently blind old beggar sitting against a wall, thrumming his feeble guitar, and uttering an occasional hoarse wail by way of singing. It is a sight which I have passed a hundred times unnoticed; but now suddenly I am arrested and seized with a voluminous unreasoning sentiment—call it pity for want of a better name. An analytical psychologist (I myself, perhaps, in that capacity) might regard my absurd feeling as a compound of the sordid aspect of this beggar and of some obscure bodily sensation in myself, due to lassitude or bile, to a disturbing letter received in the morning, or to the general habit of expecting too little and remembering too much.

Veranda Hung with Wisteria

The adoration of mountains, Mr. Poe read in Alexander von Humboldt's *Cosmos,* and the contemplation of flowers distinguish Chinese poetry from that of Greece and Rome. Ssu-ma Kuang, statesman and poet, described in his *Garden,* written around the time of the Norman invasion of England, his wide view of the river Kiang crowded with junks and sampans, the black green of the pines beyond his terrace of peonies and chrysanthemums, the blue green of the shrubbery, the red gold of the persimmons, while he expected with contentment the arrival of friends who would read their verses to him and listen to his.

Boys Smell Like Oranges

On a fine autumn afternoon in 1938 two elderly men met at the Porte Maillot, as was their habit, to walk together in the Bois de Boulogne, Professor Lucien Lévy-Bruhl, who was eighty and strolled with an easy dignity, his hands behind his back except to accompany a remark with rounded gestures, and Pastor Maurice Leenhardt, missionary and ethnographer, who was sixty, tall and white-haired, his usual long stride curbed to match the amble of his slower friend.

They knew all the paths and small roads, the playing fields and children's zoo, and each had favorites among them, the one making his choice without a word from the other.

—These Trumai we were talking about yesterday, Lévy-Bruhl said, who are known by their neighbors to sleep at the bottom of the river.

He stooped to greet and stroke a cat, causing a second and third to glide from the underbrush. Pastor Leenhardt took the occasion to light his pipe. Lévy-Bruhl held out empty hands to show the cats he had nothing to give them. There was an old woman laden with sacks who fed cats in the Bois. She was one of the regulars they met on their walks.

—Madame your friend will be along. We know that it is a waste of breath trying to explain to the Trumai's neighbors that nobody can sleep underwater. They *know* they do. The syllogism men cannot sleep underwater, the Trumai are men, therefore the Trumai cannot sleep underwater won't work.

—Perhaps, Pastor Leenhardt said, we are looking at their logic the wrong way.

—Their logic!

Footballers, their shoulders sagging, their feet heavy, straggled muddy and tuckered toward the goalposts, where they sat and lay, like tired soldiers making bivouac. Some were in jerseys so worn that the blue was slate and the red collars and cuffs pink, colors more fitting for a Chinese poet than for a French boy. Late-afternoon light burnished their hair, making flames of cowlicks. Time stood still.

The captain of the junior team, Jacques Peyrony, fifteen and a half, was pulling on his sweater when he saw that he was being spoken to by an older halfback on the senior team, Robinet, twenty-four, old enough to have been in the war.

—Went down four to one, ouch! Robinet said. I've been watching you for the last twenty minutes.

—I saw you.

Peyrony's face was gloriously dirty from being wiped with muddy hands. His hair tangled out over his ears. It spun onto his forehead from a whorl like a young bull's. He rubbed sweat from his eyelashes with his forearm. His mouth was half open with fatigue.

—So you noticed me? I like that, but didn't think you did. When you were barreling toward the touchline you gave me a quick glance as if I were a total stranger. No time for a hello, I know.

Peyrony flopped down on the grass. Robinet took off his jacket and laid it over his legs.

—Keep warm, he said. Cold muscles don't relax.

A dog who was being allowed by his person to romp galloped over to them, wagged his tail to ask if he could meet them, laughing, got called *bon bougre,* and came and sniffed Peyrony's crotch.

—*Connaisseur!* said Robinet. But to my nose Peyrony smells like oranges.

Peyrony reached across Robinet's legs, grabbed a dandelion out of the grass and ate it, yellow flower, stem, leaves, and root.

—Green, he said. Raw spinach is greener. The best part of the orange is the rind, a nibble of it with the pulp and juice.

Robinet's frank eyes watched Peyrony chewing.
—Girls suck lemons.
—It figures. Next they'll be playing rugby. Do they smell like lemons?
—We must suppose so.
—The greener the bitterer. Over there's licorice. The Bois is full of it. The young roots halfway up the stem are sweet. Apple's the best of tastes, pear next. The citrons are something else.
—Kumquats, Robinet said.
—*Vraiment*. And peaches.

Lucien Lévy-Bruhl walked with his hands behind his back. He stopped, spread a hand on his chest, and bowed to Maurice Leenhardt.
—My father, Leenhardt had said, held a fact to be the word of God.
—And your father taught science and was a geologist and, like yourself, was a Huguenot pastor?
—He respected Darwin and Lyell with the same honor he paid to whoever wrote First and Second Samuel, a history without logic or consistency, a text so archaic that it makes Homer seem as polished as Balzac. Its names and places are confused, its narrative is frequently incoherent. The narrator is concerned with effect and high drama, with the terribleness of a bloody and arbitrary god and with human nature at its darkest.
—And is also, like a fact, the word of God?
—The poetry, perhaps. The music. Its truth, as with myth and folktale, is deep inside. That is why it is so beautiful.

Peyrony searched around in a pocket and found the pulpy and gritty remains of an orange.
—For you, he said. I didn't finish it at halftime, as I ran to the *bistrot* in the woods and got half a cup of milk.
—*Half* a cup! Robinet said laughing. You're learning.
—Butted that damned kick full force with the top of my noggin, and it still hurts.
—Take an aspirin when you get home.

—Maybe. It will go away when I've showered.
—I love the way you look after yourself, goose. A week ago you had a cold which, as I remember, you proposed to cure with a good rubdown.
—So what do you think of the team?
—Anything's possible. You have them in command. And it's to your credit that several of them play better than you.
—I know that all too well.
—Is it, Lévy-Bruhl asked, that they think differently, or that they don't think at all?
—Differently, yes, and it's what that difference can tell us that makes up ethnology as a subject. In New Caledonia *I* was the difference, my wife and children and I. We were intruders. We smelled peculiar, we spoke their language idiotically. We could not guess what we symbolized to them, what threats we brought. The English hope of exporting iron kettles, pots, and pans to Russia in the seventeenth century was dashed by the Orthodox clergy, who were certain that devils inhabited these utensils. We were lucky in that needles and thread were thought wonderful by our New Caledonians, who have clever fingers and like making things. My first great gift was arithmetic. The island traders had been cheating them for years. I taught adding, subtracting, and dividing. That five from eight was always three gave them assurance that in me there was sound doctrine somewhere. Of the multiplication table they made a hymn and sang it in church.
—*Mon dieu! C'est joli, ça!*
—They know, Robinet said, that a good captain isn't always the best player on the team. And even if you fuck up as captain, they'll play well right on, regardless. When in the last quarter you stubbornly badgered at that winded player instead of making a decisive breakthrough, you can be sure that Labbé and that kid with the English hair saw how wrong you were but went along with you because you've trained them to. That's fine. What in the name of God are you doing?

—Getting some leaves to eat. I'm listening.
—Off of a tree?
—They're good. And some sweetgrass, here, and whatever this frilly weed is. Nettles are good only in the spring.
—*Le forêt de Rouvray,* Lévy-Bruhl said. The oak forest, *roveretum.* I played here as a child. Do primitive people ever play?
—What else do they do?
—Some advice, Robinet said, replacing his jacket over Peyrony's legs, throw Guilhermet off the team. He's weak. Every signal you give him, he's parked on his butt like those streetcars that spend half their trip stopped.

Peyrony chewed a leaf, staring across the level late-afternoon sun on the field.
—But he's my only friend on the team.
—Einstein in an article I've been reading says that the eternally incomprehensible thing about the world is that it is comprehensible. The years I've spent trying to comprehend the primitive mind.

Pastor Leenhardt, smiling, relit his pipe.
—Einstein! he said. Gravity, light, magnetic fields, time, history are as unintelligible still. None of these trouble the primitive mind, or even come to its attention. There are subatomic particles, the physicists say, which can be in two places at once. We have discussed the unfortunate missionary accused of stealing a Micronesian's yams. The missionary was miles away at the time of the theft, picking up his mail at the port. This would have settled the matter for a French jury. It cut no ice in the Micronesian mind.
—You are confusing two things, Robinet said poking a finger against Peyrony's nose. The discipline of the team applies to Guilhermet too. The team has one ideal, as its motto says, to do its best. So throw Guilhermet off, gently, with some tact and grace, but throw him off.
—I wouldn't like playing without him.
—How do you know? Is his being on the team to have him near

you more important than having another player who knows what he's doing?

—He stays. He's my best friend.

—You're sure?

—I'm not joking. He stays.

Robinet was quiet for awhile.

—In that case, keep a sharp eye on him. Make your friendship useful. Make him understand that he must play well, for you.

A ball, kicked by a player who had gone back to the field, was falling from high in the air toward two companions. Peyrony bounded up, as if catapulted, leapt, and caught it between his thighs and midriff, like a nut in a nutcracker. He released it to roll down one leg, balanced it on his toe, and then held his foot on it, David with the head of Goliath. He then jumped it into the air with both feet and kicked it with a solid dry *thuck* across the field, his leg at a perfect right angle to his body.

La liberté de cette jambe.

—Thought you were frazzled, Robinet said. You're worse than a dog that can't keep out of whatever fray's handy.

—It is as if the primitive mind thought with things rather than concepts and words, Pastor Leenhardt said. Our logic falls between things, and connects them, or dissociates them. We cannot believe that a young man who thinks himself ugly and unloved can become a bird and be befriended by the girl he longs for. You know the myth.

—Oof! Peyrony said. A good leg can't resist a hurdle. A leg that snaps into action and takes you along with it is a good leg.

—You've a fine leg, for sure.

Peyrony absentmindedly opened Robinet's small backpack, looking around in it.

—*Baume Bengué!*

He uncapped the tube, sniffed, and make a show of falling backwards.

—Comb, clean socks, experienced underwear, and, *tiens!* a

book, *De natura rerum* of all things. You read Lucretius at half-time?

—On the train, coming in. Speaking of which, shall we go back together?

Silence, with thought.

—I promised Maman I'd take the 6:32, and you stay later, don't you?

The rain that had been threatening began to fall as a light shower. Peyrony took his beret from his backpack. He found a twig and began to chew it.

Robinet, staring at Peyrony, paid no attention to the rain.

—I think I'll call you on your fib, he said, to see what's behind it. Just yesterday your mother told me that she never expected you before eight, or half past. I won't deceive you in keeping back that you're handing me a line.

Peyrony picked a blade of grass and ate it.

—The truth, then, he said smiling. I'd rather go back with the team.

—Than with me. And so's not to admit that, you fib. Remember last summer, when you asked me to go with you to the France-Angleterre match, and I said no, that I was going with Remond, just that, no explanation, thinking I was doing you the honor of imagining that you were above silly infatuations. There are times when I prefer to be with Remond than with you, so there are times you'd rather be with the team than with me. Absolutely natural and reasonable. But take care. You begin with a pretense of being nice, and then trickery gets into it, and then you find yourself fucking with people's feelings for the fun of it. Look, we're football players, not like those tennis players over there running in from the rain. Telling the truth is part of having a well-built body. So is letting it rain on you. Take your beret off. The rain wants to know who you are.

—Rain is a blessing, Lévy-Bruhl said, holding out his tongue to taste it. For my old bones, however, I think that copse with the benches is wise.

—Europeans rarely see real rain. They see gentle rain like this, and a cloudburst now and again. Rain in the Pacific is a season all to itself. Napoleon only thought he had seen mud when he called it the fifth element.
—The light is beautiful here. Would the primitive mind think it beautiful?
—Why not? It would be sensitive to the pleasantness you're calling beautiful light, but it would be very interested in the spirit inside this old tree, and in events that have happened here, a murder or debate or words of power said here by a wise elder.

Peyrony, throwing aside the jacket over his legs and pushing his tall socks down to his ankles, stretched out and welcomed the rain.
—Your boots, Robinet said. Do they lace up to a proper fit?
—I think so. Yes.
—A good boot must be against the foot on all surfaces, snug.

He felt his boot all over, pressing with his fingers, like a doctor palpating.
—How are your cleats holding up? They feel firm. Let me see your other foot.
—No!
—You're not really saying no, Robinet said, seizing the other leg by the ankle and inspecting the sole while Peyrony, half-angry, protested. So you're of the race of soldiers who would rather face death than dig a foxhole? Better to lose a cleat, bungle a kick, and risk fucking up a play than make a boring visit to the cobbler, is that it?

He tore the wobbly cleat from Peyrony's sole.
—Now you have to replace this boot.
—You idiot!
—Before every match line up your little shits and inspect every foot, carefully.
—What we call myth, Pastor Leenhardt said, is the very essence of the primitive mind. The logic is of things, not ideas. In First Samuel it's the honey on the tip of Jonathan's spear and lost

asses found by prophets that occupy a space we would fill with abstract nouns and verbs, or omit altogether. Unless, of course, we are poets and children.
—Not, then, an early logic but an alternative one?
—What, after all, *is* thought? And why should we French, who have given the world a Pasteur and a Voltaire, be so curious about the mentality of Trobriand Islanders?
—The mentality, ah yes.
—I play backfield exclusively, Robinet said. For an hour and a half I serve the ball to the forwards. Only that, nothing more. *I serve.* I must make up for the errors, stopping balls that have got past, converting weaknesses into strengths. It's a lively position. To block a strapping big bastard going like a cannonball before he can make trouble is to be alive. Your ordinary person in his daily round experiences nothing like it. To outwit galloping bulls in cleated boots coming at you like a freight train and come out in one piece, that's looking life in the eye. You have balls. You feel big. You're free of all the mingy littleness that makes people tightfisted and afraid.
—It's done you good, hasn't it? I mean, you're still in shape.
—I started out as a brawler, believe me, with fingers in eyes and elbows in ribs, but now I stick to the rules, like the clean English players, chest forward and shoulders squared. What's behind me is history.
—This light, this lovely light. Monet can paint light.
—These trees are a word of God. I learned that from the Kanaka. A leaf is a word. They have a tree that embodies forgiveness, and I gave its name to Jesus. They could have taken him for a word, except that he wasn't there. The tree was. Everything, *mon cher Lucien,* is a fiction we have supplied to complement nature.
—If we could know the history of gestures.

Pastor Leenhardt chuckled.

—Because people without a history have a history. There is no event without a past.

Peyrony was eating a stick.

—There was a woman sitting near me at the Rouen match last week who said to her boyfriend that you play like a cow. You do keep your eyes lowered and shift about like somebody who has wandered onto the field.
—That way I can do inside the rules all sorts of things that could count as errors, like not responding to taunts, saving my revenge for later. That was the one pleasure in the war, getting even. I forget what writer said that the Roman circus was a focussing and containment of violence. If I don't take out my aggressions on the field I'd bloody noses in the streetcar.
—But there's the saying that we should do unto others as we'd like them to treat us. It's in the Bible, I think.
—And it's wrong. Have you ever heard me complain about a player who's rough and mean? Do to others what they're doing to you. When you're on top of a return, naturally you're going to feed it to the team, and naturally you're going to feint, right? You've got Beyssac's eye, and Beyssac is the last person you're going to kick the ball to, and then you kick it to Beyssac.
—And the Red Lions always fall for it.
—*Eh bien!* Beside that little ruse we can put a phrase of Aristotle.
—Aristotle! *Merde alors.*
—Don't laugh at Aristotle. It is precisely when we seem most modern that we are imitating the past. I love sport, its training and spirit, the more for knowing that the classical world loved it. Aristotle said of gymnastics that they make a strategic mind, a healthy and prudent soul, and shape a liberal and courageous character. Aristotle would have said that of football, yes?
—He makes it all very moral, doesn't he? Where's the fun?
—The beauty of it is in the word *liberal:* an openness of spirit, an acceptance of the world. For the hour and a half of a game you're freely consenting with a male and liberal heart to all the fire and sanctions of the game. You accept that the sun goes in when it might have got in the other team's eyes, and that it blazes out when it's in ours. You accept the wind going against you and its

dying down when it might have been in your favor. You accept your team's doing the opposite of what you know is the right play.

Peyrony listened with big eyes, eating grass.

The rain was letting up. Lévy-Bruhl stood, brushed his sleeves with his hands, and nodded toward their path.

—Have you read Swedenborg? I mean, some of him.

—I see what you're thinking. The primitive in his imagination, his globes of light and angels and geometrical heaven, can be found in poets and mystics, in Balzac and Baudelaire. Do you want primitive thought to be subsumed in the enlightened mind?

—Is there an enlightened mind?

—Leonardo, Locke, Voltaire, Aristotle.

—Darwin, the two Humboldts, Montaigne, none of whom built villages that are poems of symbols and ideas, like my Kanaka.

Peyrony smeared the rain on his legs, pulling his shorts back as far as they would wad.

—Your Labbé and the kid with the English hair obeyed your signals when they clearly thought they were cockeyed. In football you accept all the unnecessary strain and fatigue of going through hopeless plays, like when I tear off after a man I know is faster than I, for the satisfaction of knowing that I did my damnedest, eh? You accept it when Beyssac makes an end run and scores, when it was I, I alone, who set up the play. You accept the referee's idiot rulings. You try to protest and Raimondou, the shit, shouts me down. He was eighteen and I was twenty-five, and he was wrong and I was right, but I was already learning the truth of what Goethe said: *an injustice is preferable to disorder.*

—Myth, my dear Lucien, is not a narrative. It is life itself, the way a people live.

Peyrony tried to wash his face with rain from the grass.

—You're merely rearranging the mud, Robinet said. It makes

you look as wild as a savage, a nice savage. Are you listening to a word I'm saying?
—Goethe the football player.
—It's in the hour and a half of the game that I know myself, you understand? I have to face all over again that I'm short of wind, that I let the ball get away from me, that I can't kick straight half the time. I also know that I'm in a concentration of awesome power, a power that's an electricity or the gift of a *daimon*, the mystery of *form*. It isn't constant, it comes and goes, without reason or rule. My legs on the field scythe down all the hours of the rest of the day. I feel like a god, I feel reborn and new-made, and know all over again that the body has a soul of its own, independent of the other.

Lévy-Bruhl and Pastor Leenhardt came to the walk along the playing fields where they could see boys resting in groups as colorful as signal flags on a ship.
—The word is the thing, Pastor Leenhardt said, or the word and thing are so inextricably together that the thing is sacred, as the word is, too. A man's word, his yes or no, is the man. A liar is his lie.
—How we participate, Lévy-Bruhl said, stopping to thrust his hands into his pockets, *how* does not matter, for there are endless ways of participating. Surely the deepest participation is entirely symbolic, invisible, unmeasurable. I'm thinking of identity under differences, my Jewishness, your Protestant grounding. Neither of us ostensibly participates in French culture in my sense, and yet, keeping the remark between ourselves, we *are* French culture.

They could see boys straying from the fields, getting up from their bivouac, stretching tall, pulling up socks, shaking hands.
—You will find, I think, Pastor Leenhardt was saying, that all thought among primitives, and perhaps everywhere, begins with a perception of beauty.
—You mean form, symmetry, a coherence of pattern. The light is even lovelier after the rain.

—The past to the Kanaka is *old light.* The light in which the ancestors grew yams and made the villages into words.
—*How many autumns will an old man see?* asks a Japanese poet.
—Twilight in New Caledonia is only half an hour. Even so, it is understood to be in four movements. The first is when a dark blue appears in the grass, night's first step. The second is when field mice awake and begin to come out of their burrows. The third is when the shadows are dark and rich and the gods can move about in them unseen. The fourth is night itself, when one cannot see the boundaries of the sacred places and there is no blame for not knowing that your foot is on the grass of the sanctuaries.

The Meadow Lark

I

The country road, macadam and narrow, went to marshes and meadows once it was out of the woods, and Patrick on his bicycle could see white flakes on a crawling sea from its last crest before it ramped down to the wooden causeway that rumbled as he pedaled over it to the long meadow beyond, between wetlands and the Baltic.

Grass and flowers, the meadow. Bronze midges and yellow butterflies. School was two miles behind him, in another world. He had got through algebra with a jiggling foot and cramp in the quick of his balls, a good sign. Algebra takes all your attention, an unravelling and a knitting, a flushing of x and y from parentheses, resolving top-heavy fractions, keeping left equal to right, and guessing got you nowhere.

Ethics had droned him into a revery of birches around a blue lake.

Slides of Le Corbusier and Frank Lloyd Wright made him as awake as he was ever going to be. And Rasmus Rask, he'd raised his hand to say he knew who he was, and got a dirty look from Sten.

He pushed his bicycle across the meadow. Cowslips and buttercups. Field violets. His wildflower book was in the saddlebags, to give him more names if he was that curious. The ones with round leaves were worts. The grasses were just as interesting. They were the algebra of a meadow.

He stood his bicycle on its stand and knelt to untie his

sneakers. His socks smelt feral, like shrews and mice, in the clean salt air. His bare feet in warm grass and on cool earth felt free.

He pulled his jersey over his head and hung it on the seat of his bike and spread his arms for the wind to lick and the sun to warm. He held his arms out and turned on his axis. If Jack were here with him, he would wonder. He would have run ahead into the meadow, sniffing close, looking up to laugh. Jack would have his run in the park when he got home. For now, he was alone, he and his bicycle, whose mode of existence was different.

He fingered loose the brass brad of his jeans, and tugged the zipper halfway down. Sten, of the long-lashed sleepy eyes, had jeans with a split crotch, so that when he sat they gaped and showed the white of his underwear. He said that girls were warm, wet, and slick inside, and smelled of fish. Sten had kissed a girl all of an afternoon, his open mouth cupped over hers for hours.

There was no one closer than the dim sailboat just under the haze of the horizon. The pod of his briefs was upped and forward. He slid his zipper all the way down and pushed his jeans to his ankles. The wind on his legs was kind and sweet. Stubborn erections were an embarrassing nuisance, springing up when you were flustered or nervous. Here, however, he was alone, and what did the meadow or sky or his bicycle care? He put his jeans over his jersey, and with a grin for his brashness and as an apology to his guardian angel, whom he trusted to understand, added his briefs. It was like opening a letter, the blue waistband was somehow the stamps and address and the deflated cavity of his briefs the envelope.

His impudent penis stood stiff, a scandal in the meadow.

Where the bicycle was, with his clothes on it and his sneakers and socks beside it, had become a territory. As long as he was near it, he could get back into his clothes quickly. Which, he said under his breath, his knuckles on his hipbones, is silly. Mama and Papa cannot see me, nor Grandmother Matilda, nor Sten nor Olaf nor Jack, who wouldn't mind but would sniff. Only God, and He knows what I look like both inside and outside, and Sten's split jeans probably don't get more than a glance of His attention. He might even be amused. That would be good to know.

Ranunculus. And everybody knows a dandelion. And that bird over there, doing back-flips in the air, is a lark.

Bravely, or impudently, the guardian angel would know which, he walked away from his bicycle, playing his foot in tufts of wildflowers and knotgrass. He smoothed his fingers on the thin nap of pubic hair that grew as slow as time in the Ethics class.

The meadow sloped toward the beach. What had seemed its flatness, green and flowery, became a mild convexity, and perspective collected the flowers into islands and rivulets of color. A sweet scrunch, as in one's back teeth when chewing a big mouthful of chocolate cake, tightened in his balls. The thrill of freedom he recognized in this proud quickening, or of transgression, the world could figure it out for itself.

He had not looked behind him to see how far he was from his bicycle and clothes. Everything had to be the same as before. His penis seemed trollish, hooded, from the order of mushrooms. As with eye and eyelid, it had its own covering, which, as before, he pulled carefully back, a congenial throb melting under his fingers, to be wholly naked. He would again walk to the far end of the meadow and take the measure of his liberty. The grass was friendly, the sunlight warm.

II

Intuition, Santayana wrote in *Skepticism and Animal Faith,* finds essence by watching, by exerting animal attention. Now when he watches, an animal thinks that what he watches is watching him with the same intensity and variability of attention he is exerting; for attention is fundamentally an animal uneasiness, fostered by the exigencies of life amid other material beings that can change and jump. Stillness or constancy in any object accordingly does not seem to an animal eternity in an essence; it seems rather a suspension of motion in a thing, a pause for breath, an ominous and awful silence.

He is superstitious about the eternity of essences, as about all their other properties. This breathless and ghostly duration which he attributes to essences, treating them like living things, is his confused temporal translation of their eternity, mixing it with existence, which is the negation of eternity.

III

Dieu reconnaîtra ses anges à l'inflexion de leurs voix et à leurs mystérieux regrets.

IV

Mice about. Green-shanked moorhens in the marsh. His warm shoulders were turning pink. The silence was a kind of music, of which the lark's whistle was a part.

Frivolling around in a field, he would answer at home, to look at wildflowers. To be outside, no need to mention outside his clothes, but maybe to speculate, Papa liked speculations, the free play of the intellect he called it, on outside and inside. The meadow was an outside, though to God it was deep inside the earth's layer of air, inside the sun's pod of sibling planets, a speck in the Galaxy. His feet liked being outside socks and shoes, his penis and scrotum liked being outside underpants and jeans.

Outside his window at home was an apple tree. It knew nothing of the desk, the books, the warm bed inside, as this meadow was blessedly ignorant of the automobiles on the road half a mile away. Did one tree know another? The lark knew the meadow; did the meadow know the lark?

Free play of the intellect is all very well, Mama would say, except that nobody on earth can answer Patrick's questions. He had asked why larks sing in a snowfall, why high notes are high, and how we can dream about places we have never been. How can we ever know what other people see and think, what other people feel? Other people are an inside in an outside. Perhaps everything's taking an outside in. For we do know, sort of, what other people feel.

He could become a botanist and take the meadow in, and an entomologist to get the insects. Photographer, painter, writer. Soil analyst, geographer, climatologist. He could camp here, maybe even with Sten, and make friends with him, and look at his beautiful eyes.

He had not played with his penis, which he liked to do when he was alone, except to unsheathe the glans, and yet it felt happy and in a willing spirit. It was a new emotion, to feel sexy because of grass between the toes, your whole body washed by a lazy wind, the sun warm on your face.

Before, only day before yesterday, he had been on his way back to his bike when the wonderfully strange feeling in his balls had stopped him. Surprise, pause, and the other surprise, the arc of sperm that bucked out in a sweet spasm.

He had jumped back, only a little frightened. Then he had laughed, in full knowledge of what was happening, and leant to find the dollop in the grass, to taste it, intelligently.

He had, with Papa's conniving complacency and Mama's studied indifference, played with himself since he was much younger, like Peder and Asgar, but with only a drop of clear dribble at the quivering tingle.

The taste was alkali, with a tinge of sweetgrass. Bewilderment and a blush turned to wonder; wonder, to a silly delight. He looked all around. The world was still there. He had hastily pulled on his jersey, and had given his penis, nodding limber, a friendly squeeze, as a promise. His body had declared a new way things were to be. He had dressed quickly, mounting his bike with a brown leg thrown high. To ride home with a secret is to ride as never before.

It wasn't as if he didn't know that nothing happens twice. It was that what makes things so interesting is that we hope they will.

And without timelessness to traverse, time could not move.

The Table

On the *trottoir* at Le Consul as was, ten years ago, not the gentrified one there now, on the Avenue Friedland, a round sidewalk table with a glass of red wine and plate of Gruyère, bread and butter, and a book, Henry de Montherlant's *Les Olympiques* in which you can read that on an autumn afternoon in 1938 the fifteen-year-old soccer player Jacques Peyrony *endosse son sweater. La sueur couvre le visage du jeune capitaine, noir de la terre qu'y laissèrent ses mains en s'y portant, y dessine des rouflaquettes humides; et ses traits sont tirés par-dessous cette patine ruisselante, et ses joues brûlent au point qu'il cligne des paupières, et il s'essuie le front avec son avant-bras. Son visage est lisse comme un galet poli, mais le front, même dans le repos, est labouré de trois rides ondoyantes, semblables aux ailes d'un caducée, ou à ces frisons hirsutes sur le frontal d'un taurillon: elles lui donnent un air à la fois gosse et sauvage, qui est l'air même des taurillons. De fatigue, sa bouche reste entrouverte, son regard est devenu terne et ses prunelles ont étrangement pâli,* after a game played, as the Dutch philosopher Adriaan van Hovendaal observed in his *Het Erewhonisch Schetsboek,* on an afternoon when the eighty-year-old Lucien Lévy-Bruhl and Pastor Maurice Leenhardt were taking one of their habitual walks through the Bois, Leenhardt who said that in the Western world movement is dead, that theology has forgotten it, but that in the bible movement is everything, no manifestation of God without it: a column of fire in the desert, a prophet convulsing the people, the Son descending to the world, His spirit flowing out, the gospels are a lively coming and going of people, and that God is love, which moves, and that it is beauty by which the idea of coherence comes together in the mind, and has not Cocteau drawn an

Annonciation Football, rhyming the Messenger with Peyrony and his *équipe*, for Calixte Delmas was an angel of grace at a time when the angel of death was hammering his black sword at the forge.

And did not Esdras say: Like as the field is, so is also the seed: as the flowers be, such are the colors also: such as the workman is, such also is the work: and as the husbandman is himself, so is his husbandry also: for it was the time of the world.

The River

We were to be interested in pine cones. That would also be stuff for the Sunday letter home. Pine cones. Parents are interested in getting a letter and don't care what it says. The weather has been fine. The eats are lots but icky. Orienteering and botany are fun. Hugo the scoutmaster tells deadweight good stories around the campfire at night. The mosquito is the national bird of Sweden. Probably best to leave out that they call me Carrot Hair Green Eyes. Christian has an ingrown toenail but not about the pus that squirts out when mashed. Or how it fizzes when Hugo pours hydrogen peroxide on it. Rasmus and Sven had a wrestling match that was something to see. It would not interest the parents that Sven is deadweight handsome or that he uses words Hugo says are vulgar. Hugo says that the trees around here and the hills and sky are landscapes. Your loving son Adam. Pine cones.

Christian said the dip in the pines was where Rasmus and Sven were going to wrestle and that we could come watch. He says it will be awful but not pukey and maybe not even scary. It's just that it's the kind of thing it's hard to explain to scoutmasters. I hate people hurting each other. Christian says it's their game. I hate fighting. In the hollow and it's not fighting.

Weymouth's pines.

They're going to wrestle. They're not mad at each other.

I ran a finger under my nose to show I was not sure I wanted to watch. But Christian is my best friend. He had asked Rasmus. Sven said it would give us a trauma or something. Rasmus said that they were timber wolves and we were cubs.

Christian said that we didn't have to go. Sven will go to the dip one way and Rasmus another as a feint. We were interested in pine cones.

Volleyball and laundry were on the bulletin board. The one I despise and the other is a drag.

The dip is pines and maybe some larches and birches on the hill slope and around. It was likely that all this just might have open britches as part of it. With Christian that was always a possibility. Because we're friends. On the trail the year before he had without a word or even a look fished out his dink and made it stiff and slipped the foreskin back and pulled it forward and asked God to witness how good it felt. So I wiggled mine out too. He looked at the sky and at his dink and at mine. He asked if I did it a lot. O yes. He slitted his eyes and whistled. The truth was once in awhile. He grinned his loving grin. We've been that kind of friends since.

Sven was already in the dip when we got there. He did not give us so much as a look or a grunt. He's like that. He was taking off his denim pants and was trim and muscled and brown all over. He stuffed his white socks into his sneakers and wore an American jockstrap from the Spejdersports Shop in Kongens Lyngeby. Papa said that even at soccer I need a jockstrap about as much as a duck needs galoshes. Fathers understand either too much or too little.

Daylight fell bright through the opening in the pines and the dip was deadweight quiet. We walked softly. Sven was studying his toes with his fingers and then the pod of the jockstrap.

Christian nudged me with his elbow and I leaned to be whispered to. A puff of hot breath in my ear. Blowing out the cobwebs.

We weren't there.

I asked if Sven's hunching his hips meant something and Christian said to ask somebody who might know. It's to show us that nobody's watching him. That we don't count. It's like in the shower. You see but don't look.

I said it was a thing you do on a skateboard to gross out the public.

Christian said that God knew. I bet He didn't. Not with Sven.

He was the tallest of us. You would not know from seeing him all but naked and staring at the ground and fitting his jockstrap neater that he plays the cello.

He has been to a Greek island.

We jumped. Rasmus had come up behind us and mussed our hair as he passed.

On these fucking pine cones? he asked Sven and got a blank gaze back.

Rasmus zipped down his jeans and kicked pine cones left and right. His hair was a darker blond than Sven's. The dip of his blue briefs showed below his tank top with the Spejder insignia on its front.

Barefoot. Sven's first word since we got there. He then said in the same level voice that he would get Rasmus's underwears off in the first three minutes.

Christian slid closer.

Rasmus asked if Sven would get his underwears off with our help. With the help of the puppies.

Nobody's here but us. We two alone. Nobody knows where we are.

Rasmus kicked pine cones and asked if there wasn't a better place. Rasmus in tank top and blue briefs you could only see the front of.

Sven began to circle. His cool gaze was something Christian and I copied. We denied it when we caught each other at it. But it was what we were doing.

Circling to attack.

Rasmus was toeing off his sneakers. Snatching at their laces while kicking pine cones. He asked if Sven couldn't wait a fuckering minute.

He was in sock feet when Sven lunged into him and brought him down backwards. I put an arm around Christian's shoulders. Rasmus locked both arms around Sven's neck and heaved with his back arched and heels dug in for purchase.

They knew how to wrestle.

Christian put an arm around my shoulders. Sven kneed himself free of Rasmus's hold and squirmed under.

Christian said it was awesome.

Sven pried his shoulder under Rasmus's chin and tried to pincer his legs around him. Rasmus was flopping like a fish. His underpants were still on. I asked Christian if there were points for that.

Just when they were thrashing and rolling like two dogs in a fight Christian darted out and started picking up pine cones. I said he would get smushed. Sven and Rasmus are fuckering crazy. He danced back out of their way. Their flailing legs almost got him.

Christian asked if you can get any stupider than wrestling in a place you haven't cleared.

Rasmus's underwears was down off his butt.

Christian said that if you twisted his ankle like that his foot would come off.

Rasmus's briefs were down to his knees. Were three minutes up? I asked.

One of Sven's balls had got out of his jockstrap. And my arm would come off if you twisted it like that.

I like their little grunts. Like pigs. Grunts are all that's allowed. Big boys don't howl. Oops! Rasmus has pulled Sven's jockstrap down. When they roll the other way. Like now. Kick pine cones out from under them. I'll help.

Christian said that if they didn't care why should we?

They were totally dirty. Leaf trash all over them. Then they fell apart gasping. Soldiers in a war film. Rasmus felt his ankle. To see that it was there. He flicked pine needles from inside his briefs and pulled them all the way on again. He looked at his skint shoulder. There was a bubble of spit between his lips. He did not look at Sven. He was breathing hard.

Sven plucked his jockstrap from around his ankles and threw it over his shoulder. He toed a pine cone to one side. Rasmus started gathering them and tossing. We moved in and helped.

Sven's face was blank as if he were about to go to sleep. There was pine trash all over it. Scary.

Before we could get out of the way Sven heaved up and dove onto Rasmus who gripped his forearms and wrapped his legs around him and rolled them both over.

Christian said Sven was a fuckering lunatic. And Rasmus another. We scuttled back to safety on all fours. There go his underwears again. O lord! but he's helping Sven take them off.

I said I wasn't following things at all and thought that it was time for us to leave. And if there's blood I've already left as soon as I see it.

Christian called on Jesus.

Sven had released his grip and gone limp. He lay on his back. Rasmus was leaning over him on hands and knees. He pried Sven's mouth open and looked in. Like a dentist. And like a doctor he ran his fingers down Sven's chest and tummy and poked his scrotum gently.

Christian looked at me. I looked at Christian. Does he think he's killed him? Doesn't look dead to me. Snurfling like a seal.

I didn't want to ask if he had a hard-on as his dick might be that big all the time. You had to see it to believe it. Christian monkeyed around to get a better look. He crept back to say in my ear that he'd heard they wrestled until they had hard-ons. But Rasmus didn't. A warning look. I nodded. We huddled closer. I'd never heard of any such.

Christian then said out loud and brightly that we could say anything we wanted to. They're not listening. We aren't here.

What it all looked like was that there was a dare. I said this out loud. Christian looked scared again. Sven was known to be stubborn with dares.

We could ask.

No we can't.

Then everything was very quiet. The ruckus was over and something else was about to happen. Rasmus pulled off his tank top. It was wrinkled and dirty and damp. He spat out a pine needle. They sat with their long brown legs stretched out and breathed through their mouths. They avoided each other's eyes.

We watched. The feeling was complete that we weren't there. We stayed close for solidarity. I had a peculiar feeling that Sven and Rasmus knew who they were and that we didn't. Everything began to lose its familiarity. Sven's nipples were as big as coins and sat in a perfect symmetry on his wide chest. The veins in his arms and on the back of his hands were swollen. And there was a fat vein along the top of his dick.

Christian kicked a pine cone and looked uneasy. Sven reached and felt Rasmus's ankle again. He slid forward and put his hands on Rasmus's knees.

Jesus got called again. Checking to see did he bust anything.

Christian said I couldn't ask him as he couldn't even guess anymore. He said this out loud.

And Sven who had been gazing at nothing in the wood turned with a lazy look to stare at me and Christian. We slid back. Sven's noticing us was casual and uninterested. But his eyes met Rasmus's. They looked at each other for awhile.

What they did next made my cheeks hot and my back cold. Sven crawled smack on top of Rasmus like a boy on a girl in the comic books. They rubbed noses like Greenlanders. Christian was all for staying but I said that if there was a time for leaving this was it.

Rasmus said that if we told this we'd have our heads knocked together.

Rabbit noses!

Sven was talking to us. Christian was getting to his feet to run but I was not certain what to do. Sven had raised up and propped himself on his elbows and had called us rabbit noses. He was still hip to hip on Rasmus and his toes were sliding along the soles of his feet like making love to them.

Are we here? Christian asked.

I said we were leaving.

Sven said that we were not.

Try and stop us.

When Sven commanded us to come closer Rasmus gave us a big friendly smile and said that everything was OK. Sven thinks your unwrinkled brains ought to know what we're doing. For your education and character. You can tell it all over camp and lower the moral tone of the whole troop. So come over.

We wiggled on our butts a bit closer but not within reach.

Sven sat up and Rasmus made a long stretch under him. Sven came back into the world and said we were going to the river to get the trash off him and Rasmus. He would tell us on the way what they were doing. But first a question for the rabbit noses to answer. What's on the other side of that hill there?

I said the camp.

Not that hill. *This* one.

I said Holstein cows all facing the same way in a pasture. And probably Asgar and Peder trying to ride them.

Sven said I was wrong. He found his jockstrap and whipped it free of leaf trash. He tossed Rasmus his blue briefs. Over that hill is a town with white buildings and red tile roofs.

I asked its name.

Do we know its name? Rasmus asked Sven. The streets are just spaces between buildings. There's a white temple the shape of a shoebox on a green hill. Its roof is held up on fluted columns. There's a market with awnings and a gymnasium and stables and blacksmiths.

Sven added dogs and chickens. In the gymnasium is a wrestling floor of fine dust. When it's not being wrestled on it's smoothed over and used as a blackboard for drawing geometry on and for writing on with a stick.

I said Athens and Sparta. Old Greeks. They wore window drapes when they wore anything at all.

Christian said they were not over that hill.

You think not? Sven asked. He hunkered to be at eye level with us.

I said we could go see. What else was there to say?

Rasmus said that at last there was a gleam of intelligence from us.

But we didn't go toward the valley over the hill but along the path all rocks and raised roots and low branches down to the river at a place we're not supposed to swim at and where there's a bateau tied to two planks for a landing out of sight in the river grass. Neither Sven nor Rasmus had a stitch on. Their armpits smelled like beer and their hair was wrecked. Rasmus was limping. Sven said he thought he had a rib slipped out of where it was meant to be. This path down to the river is probably Neolithic. Christian had got in behind Sven going down the path. I was behind Rasmus before he guided me around to be in front of him and behind Christian. You two are together.

Sven said that last summer on his Greek island two Greek boys had climbed on top of a wall around a restaurant terrace and one of them had pulled down his pants for everybody to see his dick and his friend had pointed to it while making a speech about it which nobody understood. A whopper for a kid his age.

Christian asked why.

I don't know O rabbit nose. Because he was proud of it. In the gymnasium in the white city over the hill there's a boy showing his to his admirers.

It was in Vienna that Vilhelm Ekelund saw a tree that looked like Plato.

That was Rasmus and Sven lifted his hands palms up. He said that seeing was after all everything.

A Chinese painting. The grass. The river.

Why not? Rasmus asked. We feel and we see. We are.

We could smell the river and see some of its shine through the trees. Christian asked us all if we knew that a number reversed and subtracted from itself always gives nine.

Sven said that math made his mind wander.

Christian went on. Twenty backwards is zero two. The remainder is eighteen and you fuse the one and eight to get nine. Nineteen from ninety-one is seventy-two. Two and seven are nine.

I said that twelve from twenty-one is nine exactly.

So is forty-five from fifty-four. This was Rasmus. Twenty-five from fifty-two. And you put the two and seven together to get your nine.

Thirty-six from sixty-three. There are a lot of twenty-sevens in all this.

Sven said that he had pine trash in his ears and up his nose and why was Christian doing his math homework in the wonderful out-of-doors with naked friends and a blue sky?

Christian said that is wasn't his homework but something he'd thought up himself.

You run into the best part of it when you reverse a number like eleven. You get zero. But you have to understand that all zeros are nines in disguise. Take twenty. It's two nines plus two. All numbers ending in zero are the suffix times nine plus the suffix. Forty is four times nine plus four. So when the remainder is zero it's nine right on.

You thought this up? Rasmus asked. He turned and took Christian by the ears and stared into his eyes.

Christian said that it was because of base ten. If you say base ten is *b*, then *by* plus *zed* minus *bz* plus *y* and these equal *b* minus one times *y* minus *b* minus one times *zed* which equals *b* minus one times *y* minus *zed*.

Rasmus said that Grundtvig would have hugged Christian and kissed him on the nose and served him a plate of pancakes with elderberry jam and poured the buttermilk for him.

Eighty-seven minus seventy-eight. Sven was working on his fingers. Nine on the button. Four hundred and thirty-one minus a hundred and thirty-four. What does that give? This may be sex for infants. Do numbers make your wizzle point skyward?

Two hundred and ninety-seven. Fuse to eighteen. Eight and one are nine.

When we got to the two-plank landing and the half-sunk bateau Sven waded into the river through the grass up to his hips. Rasmus followed. It was an afternoon of not knowing what comes next. So we stood with doubt and hope on the landing and watched them duck and dog-paddle and splash. Rasmus combed trash from Sven's hair with his fingers. They swam out to the current and had to kick hard and reach long to get back upstream. They stood in the shallows and knocked water from their ears. The river danced light on them. They took the bateau by its ends and emptied it.

Walt Whitman! Sven shouted.

Pythagoras! Rasmus shouted back.

Christian gave me one of his looks. Meaning that the world until this moment was lots crazier than we had known. And then Sven called me by my name. Adam Overskov. He was washing leaf trash from under his foreskin when he said it and I could feel my blush. He was standing in the river up to his balls. His brown red bush was flat wet.

Into the river with us! Rasmus said.

What's Pythagoras? Christian asked. I thought he was geometry.

Climb out of your togs. We don't bedevil rabbit noses. Christian Gandrup. He said his name too. Pythagoras as Hugo explains him was all for friends and said they're another self. That's true. But he had not read Walt Whitman and was a Lutheran and Rasmus believes him that friends should be brotherly like Epameinondas and Pelopidas and when they are together have only pure thoughts even when they're wrestling or in the one sleeping bag breathing in each other's ear unhampered by underwear or pyjamas. I'll bet Overskov has never had a pure thought in his life. I hope not.

Rasmus jouncing the bared head of his dick in the river said I'd never had any other kind nor Christian either. Sven imagines happily that everybody's as saturated with testosterone as he is from ears to heels.

Epimonides and the other his friend. Christian's voice was friendly earnest. He'd been won over.

Two Pythagoreans. Epameinondas. They live in the city over the hill there. Tall handsome fellows with Greek noses. They love each other in the friendliest of ways but their beautiful *posthoi* hang down limp or only angle out a little. Like mine.

Beautiful what? Christian grinned his question and was taking off his sneakers. His look to me was to shed what he shed.

Greek for dicks. Don't you learn anything in school? Big balls too. *Didymoi.*

This got Sven splashed by Rasmus hard and wild. And was splashed back even fiercer. Dripping and laughing Rasmus said we were to listen to about half of what Sven said. Sven was an ironist and child of Kierkegaard.

Christian was pulling his T-shirt over his head. So was I. From pine cones to Kierkegaard. And the tree that looked like Plato.

Sven said that if we had paddles and could unlock the chain on the bateau and if the bateau weren't sinking before our eyes we could go for a row on the river. Walt Whitman would like that. As things stood we could lie in the sun on the two planks and the better part of two others if there were room for two Pythagoreans and two spadgers with rabbit noses who are best friends. Aren't you?

Christian's britches off.

I said we were best friends.

Four hundred and two minus two hundred and four. A hundred and ninety-eight. Fuses to eighteen.

Nine!

Rasmus said that if we didn't get wet we can't dry in the sun. In the city over the hill they adore logic.

Christian's briefs coolly down and off. Sven held out his hands to lift him into the river where he held his nose and sank out of sight before bobbing up doing a frog stroke.

One hundred minus zero zero one. Ninety-nine. Eighteen. Nine!

What I needed was to hide in the river as my underpants were poked out by an erection which I was both proud of and embarrassed by. When Sven and Rasmus were wrestling or whatever they were doing I had been scared and humiliated or maybe only left out and bullied or all of these together and their friendliness had made me happy. Sven with a teasing smile put his fingers over his eyes and gave me a thumbs up. Rasmus not looking lifted me in.

Cold water cure.

Christian ducked me when I was near enough. I upended him by grabbing an ankle. We horsed around. We showed off. We hollered.

Time stopped all afternoon.

Sven and Rasmus sat on the landing planks toe to toe with their arms crossed on their knees and their chins on their forearms golden naked in the summer sun. Blond naked. They made room for us dripping and joshing. I think we waked them from something they do with their eyes. I'd swum naked lots and run around on beaches but I'd never sat and talked as close as puppies in a basket. Christian gave up trying to be modest when Rasmus said that boys are unreasonably shy and I sat as he did with his tight pink balls and pinker dick sticking pretty much straight out.

Sven said we were nicely equipped as boys and Rasmus lying back with his legs alongside Sven's said to the sky that we'd be depraved by Sven and Walt Whitman in under ten minutes. Nothing to do with him. Ninety-six minus sixty-nine is twenty-seven. Nine again.

It always will be.

Christian asked how we were to be depraved. I said we were already. Rasmus put his hands over his face.

The backwards numbers are something like multiplying a number by one through nine and fusing the integers. Take six.

Six times one is six. Six times two is twelve. Six times three is eighteen. Twelve fuses to three and eighteen to nine. That six three nine remains on out to infinity.

Rasmus worked out the next six three nine in whispers to himself. Christian did six times seven and eight and nine out loud.

Rasmus said that despite the brilliant conversation Sven was studying our accessories while seeming not to. God in his inscrutability made him that way.

Christian said he didn't mind.

Adam's looks like a lizard that's swallowed a wren's egg.

Rasmus said he was doing seven. What is the pattern?

The seven is at the beginning. The eight is in the middle. The nine is at the end. All these patterns end with nine. Five and three and one come between the seven and the eight and each is two less than the one before. The same for six four two between the eight and nine.

And five is two less than seven. But why in the world is there a jump from one to eight in the middle?

Because there's a hidden seven in there.

Sven running his finger around his navel said that he liked Christian's ribs and toes and that maybe he'd make two new friends while keeping Rasmus the true blue Pythagorean as his best friend with gritted teeth. We wrestle when I can't stand it. Pythagoreans draw triangles together and sing logarithms and hug and kiss just like Lutherans but they activate south of the belt to give business to the stork only.

Rasmus said it was safe to believe one half of that.

Christian blushed and said that he was so confused he might as well be dreaming.

I said that went for me too.

Sven said he was not being confusing at all. He assumed that we kept our adorable little dinks happy.

We said yes together. Mine twitched.

Sven said that was a start and that he now had two new

friends who raise guinea pigs and newts and sail the streets on five-speed Swedish bikes and collect stamps and think Vivaldi and Busoni are racing cars and are diligent and conscientious sliders down of their jeans zippers.

Rasmus raised up to look. To wrinkle his nose at Sven and to look at Christian and me with a sigh and a smile. A sighing smile.

He said as he lay back down that over in the white city they would write poems about us and give us roosters and knucklebones but that we would still draw triangles and sing logarithms and hold our mother's hand in the market.

Sven said we would be just as good friends and that time was as green now as it was then. Ask Walt Whitman.

Rasmus sat up and said he was going to explain everything. Not until he was through were we to speak. Then we could talk until we gibbered. He told Christian to stay where he was and picked me up by the armpits as if I weighed nothing and sat me down between Christian's legs facing inward. Deftly he placed my arms over Christian's shoulders and Christian's over mine. He said to touch noses. Our dicks nudged each other.

We both began words which Rasmus silenced. Hug if you want to and kiss if you want to and it's fine if your dicks rear up according to nature. I thought this up for Sven and me summer before last when we were on trail in a larchwood in Norway. We looked into each other's eyes for how long who knows for time stops. I figured it out. A long togetherness with a promise to each other to let the craving build and build and not give in.

Sven said that if anybody thought he had a crazier best friend he'd lose his shirt on the bet. And it was only fair to say that they do give in when they're both out of their minds and Rasmus mopes the next day about lack of character and about Pythagoras's noble soul.

Now you can talk.

We stayed as we were blowing our breaths back and forth and running our fingers around each other's ears and Rasmus twisted Sven's arm and pushed him in the river and dove in after him and we could hear them singing logarithms and drowning each other until after a long while they were back spilling the whole river over us out of their hair and talking about peanut butter and banana sandwiches with cold goat's milk and time began again.

Concert Champêtre in D Minor

DENIM WITH RED STITCHING

Fru Overskov had looked at the jeans with disbelief and awe. They would have to be soaked in one detergent before being washed in another. Grease, mud, sand, grass, and nameless stains vegetable and mineral.

—They do sort of stand by themselves, don't they? Adam observed. And smell like the zoo.

—Feral, yes.

—The green on the underpants is pond scum.

—Is this Jeremias still looking at your comic books?

—Peter is helping him. He doesn't read so well.

—There is a God, because there are mothers.

ELEVENSES

—Our root problem, Rasmus said to Fru Overskov over coffee in the kitchen, is baseness, lack of character. He won't corrupt Adam and Christian, who are irrevocably civilized, and certainly not Peter, whose heart is pure. You buy him shirts, which he goes and sells. He lies like an actor. He steals. All I have to stand on in this slipperiness is his emulation. He's beginning to use words he says Adam uses, like *conspue.*

—Great Lord! said Fru Overskov.

—And *geological epoch.*

MOTHER AND SON

—Well, Adam said, I got wet. It rained. I was trying to dry my underwear on a stick over the campfire. That's why the singes and the smoke smell and the specks of trash.
—Why would anybody be a mother?
—As for my hair, Christian gave me a haircut with his scout knife. Sort of sawed at it, didn't he?
—Let's move on to your knee.
—Well, we were climbing a tree.
—Your finger.
—Hugo wrapped it. I was sewing a button back on. Hugo's very particular about sewing back on buttons, and I stuck the needle through it.
—Stuck the needle through it.
—Yes.
—As for the comic book that Tropsfører Tvemunding thinks just might be a bit advanced for your years, that's your affair. I don't pry. There are parents who open their children's mail and snoop in their diaries and eavesdrop on their phone conversations.
—I can never keep a diary going.
—And listen to tattle. But I am not a barbarian. You can correspond with the Bishop of Greenland. We won't even ask you how his bunions are in January.

WHITE SOCKS

Smelling of yeast, of sourdough.

TERRITORY

Of which Pastor Ingeborg, looking in on Peter after tea with Mama downstairs, said was an interesting subject, taking it up from the biology book on the desk without comment on the comic book next to it, all beings having an exquisite sense, possessiveness, and defense of their places, there being nothing so tragic as dispossession, as witness our primal parents and the Jews and the American Indians. Peter and Adam's room seemed to him to be a charming example of a shared territory, a nest of friendliness, childhood being a kind of paradise, so to speak. But Pastor Ingeborg was not born yesterday and imagined, with a smile, that even here, in a room so rich in books, maps, sporting gear, posters, flowers in a windowbox, twin beds friendlily side by side, there was the occasional, certainly not frequent, dispute over territoriality, but perhaps not, given the evident good nature of them both, and the excellent upbringing they were blessed to have from such accomplished and charming parents.

At which Peter beamed and nodded and replied *O jo!* while wondering about the dense ignorance of pastors, for what could witless grown-ups know of, say, the territoriality of beds, the deprivation of no longer sleeping with Adam, or of the wallow in one bed or another before the mandated time for sleep, the exact measuring of time before he could slip into Adam's bed, too soon and you got pushed out, or how long he could stay there, as Mama did sigh with exasperation when she found them in the same bed in the morning, or how to know when Adam, self-righteously in his bed with the covers up around his ears and his back to Peter and quickly asleep, would suddenly decide to join him, all long legs and knees and elbows and nudging nose and whoofs in his ears and liberal hands and lovely whispered talk about things Pastor Ingeborg had never heard of.

UNDERPANTS

Purchased by Fru Gandrup at Daells Department Store for her son Christian, size small, white combed cotton with a blue elastic waistband, *fabbricato in Italia,* transitorially in Adam's possession, by friendly swap or affectionate loan, the appropriation having been made in a birchwood where they had propped their bicycles to have a complicated conversation about geography, the moon, the rings of Saturn, the Swedish royal family, owls, and submarines, and to practice Pythagorean restraint by standing front to front with open jeans and lowered briefs, genitalia contiguous and snug but with varying accuracy of address due to vagrom throbs and slippage, hugging amicably, continuing the conversation, encouraging each other to heroic endurance, and wondering, at least by Christian, if any Pythagorean had ever done any such, or even Sven and Rasmus, with Adam saying he didn't think so, but that the idea was to put off for as long as you can something you're going to deny yourself anyway.

THE ELF

Could be heard gibbering in the thin silences of deepest night. He wore a red overcoat. He tied knots in their hair, snarled their shoelaces, jammed zippers, stole socks, sneezed under the bed, rewrote homework with wrong spellings, filched buttons. His presence was by signs not sight. Like Diogenes he lived like a mouse, eating nibbles from the refrigerator and pantry, from rucksacks before hikes. He stood on noses when you were asleep, turned water on that had been conscientiously turned off, whispered in ears. One of his specialties was leaving comic books not for the casual eye lying around.

SLEEPING BAG

When there had been snow one afternoon in waves and quanta like light with a flour of sleet whoofing around in it, Adam pulled his sweater over his head by the cushioned settle by the large window, folding it into a square, followed by his shirt, rolled, undershirt squared, jeans folded, socks flat, and briefs in a wad on top of the stack. He had hugged his mother after shaking snow from his parka, unlatching and pulling off his boots. It was after crumbling four ginger cookies into a glass of

milk to drink, chewing, that he fetched his father's sleeping bag, not his down light waterproof flat zippered scout's *sovepose* but a canvas quilt lined with fleece that snapped together. To his mother's *the snow is beautiful but awful* he smiled happily and to her *God knows where Peter is* he waffled a hand.
—Your name *is* Adam, his mother said.
—Nothing's neater than being snug and out of your clothes in the family camping sleeper, with the snow to watch, and what's the right book?

Though my little *periagua* was finished, yet the size of it was not at all answerable to the design which I had in view, when I made the first; I mean, of venturing over to the *terra firma,* where it was above forty miles broad; accordingly, the smallness of my boat assisted to put an end to that design, and now I thought no more of it. But as I had a boat, my next design was to make a tour round the island; for as I had been on the other side in one place, crossing, as I have already described it, over the land, so the discoveries I made in that little journey made me very eager to see other parts of the coast; and now I had a boat, I thought of nothing but sailing around the island.

For this purpose, that I might do everything with discretion and consideration, I fitted up a little mast to my boat, and made a sail to it out of some of the pieces of the ship's sail, which lay in store, and of which I had a great stock by me.

Having fitted my mast and sail and tried the boat, I found she would sail very well. Then I made little lockers, or boxes, at either end of my boat, to put provisions, necessaries and ammunition, etc., into, to be kept dry, either from rain or the spray of the sea; and a little long hollow place I cut in the inside of the boat, where I could lay my gun, making a flap to hang down over it to keep it dry.

I fixed my umbrella also in a step at the stern, like a mast, to stand over my head, and keep the heat of the sun off of me like an awning; and thus I every now and then took a little voyage upon the sea but I never went far out, nor far from the little creek; but at last being eager to view the circumference of my little kingdom, I resolved upon my tour and accordingly I victualed my ship for the voyage, putting in two dozen of my loaves (cakes I should rather call them) of barley bread, an earthen pot full of parched rice, a food I eat a great deal of, a little bottle of rum, half a goat and powder and shot for killing more, and two large watch coats, of those which, as I mentioned before, I had saved out of the seamen's chests; these I took, one to lie upon, and the other to cover me in the night.

CONFERENCES

—Oh, I'm awful, Rasmus said. I like to wash him. I was always the one who liked polishing the silver at home. My scouts know me to be a Tartar about hygiene, spit and polish, safety, honor, morals, and wild good health. They are also aware, at least Adam and Christian are, of Sven's and my prolonged post-adolescent golden friendship, and that he and I are of opposing minds about how friends should be friends, Jonathan and David in khaki pants and ribbed knee socks.
—The loyalties of friendship, said Fru Overskov. I think you're right. Meanwhile, I'm learning how to break fingers and how many notes to sneak from a wallet so it doesn't look like any are missing.

POSTER

Forty centimetres wide, sixty centimetres long, *een vierkleuren fotoposter*, from Amsterdam, thumbtacked at its four corners to the wall between the rack of bookshelves and the chest of drawers, reading across its top in Bayer sans serif BAAS IN EIGEN BROEKJE, depicting two naked blond handsome well-formed frank-eyed boys, one with an arm over the other's shoulders, both prepubescent but with incipient hopeful microfuzz apparent. Their father said it was their assurance that somewhere somebody understood how things are.

POSTER

On the inside of the closet door, forty-two by sixty centimetres, also *vierkleuren,* reading JONG GELEERD and with a text they had only a vague sense of, being ignorant of Dutch, depicting a mop-haired blue-eyed boy whose jeans and briefs he has shoved down to midthigh and who with thumb and two fingers has drawn back the foreskin of his erect and upcurved penis.

NIGHT

The tabret of the elf.

LATE AFTERNOON

Long slats of mellow light on the wall, across the world map. Oblong lake of light on the rug. Digital clock winks and changes a number. A spider in the back corner of the closet knits its web.

THE DOOR

Mama knocked if the door were closed, asking if she could come in, not knowing what she might not see, Papa sometimes, when he remembered, Adam never. So Peter on his bed playing with himself kept at it, with a whistle as to how sweetly it was going, when Adam and Christian tromped in from soccer silly and rumpled, in sock feet, muddy shoes in hand. Hallo Peter! they both sang, and Christian, leaning to watch, said what a respectable pink-knobbed dink Peter had, with balls as tight as as nectarine. What, he added, if we hadn't been us? We're allowed, Adam said, stripping for a shower. Let's get the mud out of our ears and what we can of it off our knees. Mama says we shouldn't invite her in when we need privacy. Papa calls it trotting the mouse and says it's not nearly as good as it's going to be. Shower together, *jo?* It's friendlier.

LE MONTGOLFIER À VAPEUR JULES VERNE

—Would you, Quark said munching an apple, look at this?
—Another printout, Buckeye said, reading aloud. HIZQIYYA TO OBS BALLOON SEGO DICE OUNCE REF MINIM PERCEP FIELD IN RE WITTGENSTEINS ELEMENTARY PROPOSITION HOPELESSLY WRONG EXPLAIN EYE REPRO COURAGE SYNERGY.
—Wad it up and throw it away, over the side.
—Rasmus is learning. They'd say *but that isn't the way we see,* and they'd be right.
—Maybe he'll learn from Jeremias how to see around corners, and in the dark, and have eyes in the back of his head.

BADEDRAGT

A *slips* is a necktie, but in France a *slip* is a bathing suit so exiguous and little and minimal that it's a seat to cover some of your behind and a cupped incurvature in front for *swans* and *pung* with a neat thin lining, trademark Hom, deadweight expensive but a gift from Papa, as Adam had talked about it covetously, dove gray with an orange waistband, a gift handed over in the car when he and Papa were going for a dip in the indoor heated pool promises had been made to take him to despite Mama's doubt that he was old enough to go there. But it was confusing in that one doesn't wear anything at all at Papa's health club, not in the glassy green heated pool with a glass roof over it and strangers talking, soaking, swimming, and sitting on the edge. We don't like strangers, do we? Papa had said, knowing Adam to require familiarity in people, or nothing doing. So be cool, you and I are together, and though I may have to speak to one friend or another, I am your friend while we're here. Fold your clothes in my basket. You can wear the scandalous French *cache-sexe* sometime soon. We all want to see you in it, and Peter can have one if he shows any interest or if there's a size for him. And there they were, bare-ass naked, and with an erection threatening, and a diving board much too high, and hairy men and men with lots of stomach, and two teenage boys who looked like Swedes. But it wasn't sexy at all, and there were strangers everywhere, and it would have been an awkward time except for the shower with Papa beforehand, together, and Papa's sitting beside him on the pool's edge after they'd swum, Papa back and forth the length of the pool, Adam side to side at the shallow end, Papa's hand on his shoulder. Did he regret coming, after all the hints he'd dropped to be brought along? Well, no, not regret, but it's not what I thought it was. It's sort of noisy and the water must be half chlorine and maybe people look better in clothes after all. And Papa had said that what he meant was that lean brown Scouts and age-mates look good stitchless, but not bankers and real-estate brokers. And Adam had said that Papa looked good stitchless, and how old was he? Twenty-nine. I begot you when I was seventeen, and you were ravishingly wonderful to beget, and Peter too. Speaking of whom, they were to pick him up at his knot-tying or dog-hair weaving or whatever it was, and they were all going out for supper, Mama being at a committee, and Peter would doubtless eat backwards, wearing the Phrygian bonnet that fathers allowed and mothers didn't, from a banana split to a pizza with anchovies and olives. We can see you in your French skimpies first thing when we get home.

CONFERENCE

—Actually, Fru Overskov said, I think the comic books are from the Lutheran synod. For all their graphic explicitness, they are suspiciously cautionary.
—All experience moves on moral ground.

—Peter reads them to Jeremias, who challenges and corrects words that I then get asked about. I don't eavesdrop. Children have voices ten times louder than adults. The Swedes can probably hear them.

NORTHERN MEADOW WITH WILDFLOWERS

Between *The Birds of Israel* and *Spejderliv* on the lower bookshelf, *Fjällflora*. Halloo! Christian on the meadow's rise to Peter toward the horizon of birches in runnels of wildbright seaming painted sedge and to Adam over by the boulders lichened greengold and spritted in silver, the sky high afternoon blue, far apart enough to be hollow voices to each other, in clear view.

Christian's summer unbarbered hair tumultuous and Shetland over eyes, over ears, his nutbrown nose peeling after a week on the trail, Hugo and a pod of the freckled and skinny cubs, half crazy with geology somewhere back down the slope, the rest off orienteering and darting about like snipes. Christian signalling stay where you are, unbuttoning. Why? Watch.

Grouse sedge wind ruffled. Christian unbuttoning.

Ripstarr. *Ullvide.*

Adam looking for mouse nests and ant kingdoms and maybe *pysslinger* the size of thumbs, ignoring Christian's predictable unpredictability, nevertheless unbuckled his belt, as Peter was tugging down his short blue pants with one hand and waving his cap with the other, Peter in thick white socks falling down rumpled, standing in woolwillow and Icelandic buttercups, *O jo!*

Do what? Adam semaphoring when he saw that Christian was all but naked and by hauling his shirt over his head, was naked, and that Peter was trying to take his little blue pants and underwear off over his hiking shoes and couldn't.

A pale yellow butterfly.

Clothes, Adam said to ants, are for carrying things. He called through cupped hands to Christian, who was peeing an amber arc, to witness how Peter doesn't know what to do with his shoes and socks. His own pants bore a canteen, Swiss Army knife, compass, and bandana knotted around the belt, never mind all the good things in the pockets. He walked bare-chested toward Christian.

Sweet air, meadow flavored.

Peter was hauling his shoes, clothes, and haversack, dropping a sock and in picking it up, his briefs. An elf moving his household goods.

A triangle, Christian said. If we keep this distance we can move about as a triangle over the meadow. Any point can move, and the others follow. Christian's *swans* is up, Peter said, and what's the triangle for?

It's because I love you, could be, you know?

Butterflies.

Peter thought about it, scratching his knee. Midges. I love Adam, Peter said, don't I, Adam?

CONFERENCE

—There's no not sleeping with him, Rasmus said. He'd never seen pyjamas, and carefully and silently watched me buy him two pairs before saying that he wouldn't wear them. When I did talk him into putting them on, he kept looking at them as if I'd made him put on a dress. In any case he took them off as we were turning in. He said he didn't want to get them wrinkled.

—You're enjoying all this, aren't you? Fru Overskov said. So am I.

GODNATBESØG

Papa grinning. Could he visit? Mama was writing against time. Not to read a bedtime story, no, but to be friendly on so weathery an evening, with clouds from Lapland, in a warm room full of sons. In his paisley short kimono with crimson belt dangling and jockey briefs fresh from the dryer, hair damp. What were they reading? And Peter could only trot his mouse so many times a day, nature being what it is.

—But, Adam said, making room on his bed and folding his arms around Papa's shoulders, what do you call times when there's no stopping and starting? Don't tease, Peter said, catapulting over to canter across Papa's thighs, balancing like a gymnast and rocking. Tell us again about how Frank Lloyd Wright leaks and Le Corbusier cracks and falls to pieces and Rogers and Piano have to be painted all the time like the Golden Gate Bridge and Mies's tall glass buildings have to be washed from the top down by men on a rope. Adam and Christian trot their mouses too.

—If Adam were to give him some space on Papa's person, Peter could walk up Papa, carefully, from knees to shoulders, and don't pull my ankles. Papa said he'd hold his ankles, and guide, and step lightly from hipbones to ribs. Small steps. Did you know that both of you were born with erections? The nurses giggled. The doctor said it's quite common, nature trying out one of her systems then and there. Easy, easy.

—Feel your heart under my right foot. Through the hair.

Shoulders. Looking down, Papa looking up. The seam in Peter's scrotum was like that in an Athenian oil bottle of the sixth century. Athlete's olive oil with dill flavoring, bottle in the shape of what I'm gazing up at, helplessly, a little boy's lizard and pair of eggs. Peter's show great promise.

—Sven and Rasmus in our scout troop know lots about Greeks. They look like Greeks. Rasmus's was as big as Papa's already. He and Sven are the best of friends, in love with each other. They don't do anything, you know, as they say being in control of yourself is good character. So they behave, leastways they say they do. They should meet Peter and blush for a week.

Papa said he knew Rasmus's father and aunt.

Peter, swinging one leg and pivoting on the other, jumped to the floor, bouncing. Kneeling, elbows on the bed, his head through Adam's legs who had renewed his hug with one arm and was edging down his pyjama pants to be Ariel, as Papa was saying that Peter was a sweet elf as he helped him off with his pyjama top, but that Adam was Ariel out of Shakespeare, or Cherubino in Mozart, Gunnar Rung's Ariel at the Brandes Center, lifted with his thumb the waistband of Papa's briefs, saying that the hair that's a doormat on your chest and runs down your middle and spins around your belly button goes on down into your bush here in your underwears, and I'm as bald as a baby from my eyebrows south. Adam is getting some fuzz. How can I take my top off if Adam has me in a scissors hold? But he can't get his bottoms off, either. He has a seam, too.

—If the knot of scamps untied, Papa said, they could depyjama and be friendlier and more Danish, unsleeving from his kimono.

—There's a story, Papa said with an amused eye to Adam who was asking with a look if he might relieve him of his briefs, in which an older brother disguises his love for his younger brother as teasing and tormenting, as he's grown into the stage when his affection and his being marinated in testosterone run into each other and he's noticing girls and shaping his muscles and has hair in his britches, and lust, vanity, and love have taken him over for their own. Well, all this happens in the story.

—Who wrote this story? Adam asked.

—Never mind. Little brother is miserable. He's hated and despised. He doesn't understand it at all, as he and his brother had been best friends. The story, however, is a wise one, and Big Brother has the brains and heart to see that it's his adolescence he's afraid of. He decides not to be afraid of his wide-awake and omnidirectional arousals. So he includes Little Brother, and his friends, and companionable girls, and Swedish comic books.

Papa, it was Peter's opinion, had made this story up.

—But, Adam said, I do love Peter.

—The story is about what's ahead.

So watch. How to hug a little brother and be climbed and

straddled. Erika has let me feel her breasts and a girl who's a friend of Carlotta's pulled her panties down for Christian, Poul, and me one afternoon, for a good look, very educational. It was OK, as Carlotta was with her and said she could do it. We sat in a line on the ground with her in front of us.
—*Frelseren,* Papa said.
—So I'll love Peter and even help him treadle his dinkum when his hand gets tired, and love Mama and Papa, and whoof in his hair, like this, even though he's shy. Why is it OK to swim and sunbathe naked but not in the house?
—Custom, Papa said, and propriety, but if you think it's friendlier.
—It's to be all alike, Peter said.
—Hug your brother, Adam, kiss him on the ear, and pass him over.

CONFERENCE

—Have you any idea, Fru Overskov asked Rasmus, what dialect Jeremias speaks? He says he doesn't want to talk like snobby people, and yet, as you've observed, he's coming more and more to talk like Adam and Christian.
—He used the word *exquisite* the other day, of a tomato and mayonnaise sandwich. I asked him where he heard it, and he said it's one the Life Guard uses a lot.
—What danger is the Life Guard?
—I don't think we can deal with that. It will run its course. Jeremias's biology is from before the Fall. For excellent reasons, I'm certain, Yahweh deprived our primal parents of a childhood. If they'd had one, however, they could have taken lessons from Jeremias. Spinoza's *natura naturans* isn't in it. Rousseau would have fainted.
—Adam, Christian, and Peter?
—Jeremias says they don't know nothing about nothing, and wonders if they're human.

A POSTER

Depicting in the innocent blue sky of Denmark *le montgolfier à vapeur Jules Verne,* or Aerostat Julius Primavera (a philological conversation with Rektor Hugo Tvemunding having decided, for the elegance of it, that *vernus,* a slave born on the estate, can just as well descend from *springtime*), in which Tumble, age 10, in a Finnish sweater, Norwegian scarf, and American jeans, sat with one arm resting along the tiller, the other on Quark's shoulder, kneading it.
—The Matabeleland Fig Tree Eobacteria fossils, Quark said. Prokaryotic. Something else. Three billion years back. Why does Hizqiyyah keep hypostasizing us as quasipubescent males?
—He knows it feels good.
—Orders from inside, more likely. Once you're into stuff, for the usual while anyway, exploding stars and the big spin and cat's cradles of phlogiston strings, with time at a set speed except where it goes crazy out near the edge, and with space for a fill, the interesting things are the wigglers, but I wish when we go into stuff naked as newts, having to steal our gear and eats, they'd have been more up-to-date than a steam balloon.
—From the time of Mozart.
—From a story by Willem Bilderdijk.
—Edgar Allan Poe.
—Jules Verne.

EIDERDOWN

Tousled hair and snub nose at the pillow end, a small tan foot with curled toes at the other. Peter asleep on his left side. Adam, awake at the gray of dawn, chilly under his coverlet, slid out of his bed and into Peter's, checking with a blind feel that our little brother's hand was where he expected it to be, cupped around his mouse.

CONFERENCE

—Tactics, Rasmus said. You will have to be very open-minded. We can't pluck Jeremias out of his world, which would be a kind of kidnapping. He stays with me when I can catch him. He stays with the Life Guard. You and I feed him. He abides Adam and Christian, and has his days of liking them immensely. It's going to be a matter of winning him over.
—I've tried table manners, Fru Overskov said, looking at the ceiling. I chatted casually that knowing things was easier than ignorance in lots of simple, everyday things. The sailor his knots and lines, the soldier his drill, and a young man his table manners. I said that our rule with Peter and Adam has been that while you're learning something it's the most important thing in the world until you've made it second nature. We made a game of it, with a card table and cutlery and plates. A slab of carrot cake was the beefsteak. I was inspired to say that this was a swap: he's to teach me something for everything I teach him.
—And what, Gertrud, have you learned?
—How to shoplift at the Irma.

TENT

Aluminum frame blue nylon Spejdersport, occupancy two, capable of zoning out the bleakest bracken waste in Sweden. Lamplit, homey, and partly dry. Warmth provided by friendship. What with the wolf's silver eyes watching from the bracken and mosquitoes in death squadrons droning in from the lake and Christian with a white blister on his heel and the night milky dark like a transparent fog and with their tent up almost out of sight of the next one, playing at survival by twos, but not quite, as Sven knew where they all were. Rasmus had said cheerfully that he wasn't worrying, as we little buggers were cleverer than him and could fend off the Russian army and make bears cringe and badgers flee, never mind creeping yellow slime from outer space. Asgar and Peder were off to our left, Tom and Poul God knows where. The locals on the train would never buy another ticket without checking to see if scouts with packframes the size of refrigerators were expected.

At their first halt, studying the map, calling the compass a joker, stretching kinked muscles, Christian and Adam pushed their jeans fronts together while looking at each other's eyes.

—Why is it silly? Rasmus asked Asgar who said it was. They're friends, they're experimenting. I thought only particular and liberated friends had volunteered. Foreplay nasty and abandoned, Sven said. It's nature and it's fun. OK, Asgar said. I'm as liberal as Peder, but no liberaler. Ha, said Peder.

—*Spejderlyst,* or *hvalpseks,* Sven said, is more exciting if it's huggermugger and outlaw. Poul and Tom come over to my place when their honest heads are turned by the god Eros, disguised for Tom as Poul groping his balls through his jeans and smiling slitty-eyed, and disguised for Poul as Tom zipping down and crossing his eyes, pushing each other onto my bed, throwing their clothes in all directions. When I was their age, anything and everything tripped the spring in my cock. Helping a kid I scarcely knew fix the chain on his bike yellowed the sheets three times, maybe four.

The bracken.

The dirty gray of the lake on out into sagging fog drifting.

We had our tent up, looking snug and homey, and there was supper to get, though I opted for dried apples.

—This motherless fire, Christian said, is all smoke and stink. Why can't we all eat together, with Rasmus cooking and a fire that burns.

The view in all directions was spooky, a dwarf forest, a hawk sitting in a dead tree.

—Scary, Christian said.

—Creepy, depressing, and wholly uncalled-for. I'm remembering the birch groves of last summer, with a moss floor, blue skies, sparkle water in the lake, all of us bare-assed brown and healthy. We sang and horsed around.

—Horse around here and you sink out of sight in a bog. Keep blowing on the fire with the tube. Put the frying pan right on the sticks and leaf gunk. Bread, cheese, butter. Patience and a burnt finger or two, and we'll have grilled cheese sammidges.

—With olives. I brought olives.

—Things are looking up. That's the nape of my neck you're whoofing.

—Don't we have a mosquito net built into the front of the tent?

—In a seam, with snaps, truly neat. Why don't you want bugs in with us? What do you have against bugs? The bread is toasting, by St. Olaf, and I think the cheese is melting. There'll be some ashes, enriched with Strontium 90 from the workers' paradise. Good for you.

With their chocolate bars they began putting clothes in the back of the tent, shoes and socks handed in by Adam, jeans, shorts, shirts, underpants, it being easier to undress outside.

—Don't bring bugs in with you. I've peed on the fire. Is the light out here summer mist or the kind of sick twilight they have around these parts?

—Look what the lamp does to the inside. We've fiddled with each other all day. Why is it sexier to slip my hand inside your shirt on the train and stick my tongue in your ear on the trail, and give each other wicked looks, than tucked up here together dressed in nothing but lamplight and not a moral between us?

—Horse apples. Rasmus and Sven are probably squeezing each other breathless, panting, and saying Greek poetry. Do you hear something?

—A bear.

—Mosquitoes dragging Asgar to their lair in the fens.

—Peder wouldn't let them. What do you suppose those two do?

—Asgar keeps himself in a trance in class by playing with his dick through a hole in his pocket. His sweet look that so charms Sigurjonsson, those beaver teeth in the round parting of his lips, the cutesy mop of hair, hiding his horns, is from being one of those Greek goat halflings. Pans.

—Fauns. *Skovguden.*

From outside, a meter or so away, Sven's quiet voice. Adam? Christian? How's it going with you scamps?

—Ho! Sven?

Looks lovely in there, Sven said, his face at the mosquito net. Sperm all over you and the tent, is there? Everybody else's lanterns are out, slurping noises only, and mooing.

—Come in out of the mosquitoes and fog, the vampire bats and owls.

—Can I? You seem to be rather occupied with each other.

—Well, some friendly loving, which, if it stays this good, we intend to keep up until around noon tomorrow, or losing our minds, whichever comes first. You can write it in the log: Overskov and Gandrup jacked each other off all night and part of the next day, we'll tell you how many times if we can still count.

—Very companionable, Sven said. *Agape* in harmony with *eros.* He was wearing a cotton undershirt he'd outgrown and frayed briefs worn thin in the pouch.

—Rasmus sent me round to see how many of you have been eaten by bears. See you at noon, then, tongues hanging out and eyes unfocussed. You smell good.

FATHER'S LEATHER JACKET

August Overskov's zippered jacket, as worn by aviators and the philosopher Wittgenstein, promised to Adam such time as it will fit him. It has weathered winters, the chilly apertures of spring, the freedom of summer, and autumn's calm recall of time. It is, as the Japanese say, *wabi,* an accustomed and familiar garment, as comfortable as a sock. Of an evening Adam likes to wear it over a household nudity, its sleeves coming down over his hands, its waist almost to his knees. Goatskin as mottled brown as an oak leaf in November, its silk lining has endured. Gliding his arms into the softness of the sleeves, Adam savors its comfort, maleness, and authority. The tribal blanket, his mother says, and that if he catches his foreskin in the zipper she will have to look to Peter for grandchildren. And why did he wear it over nothing else? It's like the sleeping bag. The good of it is to have it next to you all over.

GOD

Who is and isn't, remoter than the farthest stars and yet inside us, whose habitat is neither space nor time which he built, builds, and unbuilds as our place and its days, an event in a continuum which may in other depths of being have stranger plies of space and different speeds of time, or several times at once, with spasmodic reversals in which an old bear might suddenly be a cub, or nothing, and flow back and forth in the white light of six moons from senility to infancy.

POSTER

Showing the Luftschiffe Royal Vauxhall Nassau which, piloted by Charles Green and with The Hon. Robert Holland, member of Parliament, and Thomas Monck-Mason as passengers, sailed on the 7th and 8th of November 1836 from Vauxhall in London to Weilburg in the Duchy of Nassau, 480 miles in eighteen hours. Pear-shaped, the Royal Vauxhall Nassau was made of two thousand yards of white and crimson silk sewn in alternating gores, holding 70,000 cubic feet of gas. Rechristened The Great Nassau, she saw service for thirty-five years under the captaincy of Henry Coxwell.

POSTCARD

Recto, five tow-headed scouts each nine-tenths naked in slight *badebukser* on rocks in the shoals of a green river, stunted subarctic birches on the shore behind them. *Verso, kære* Adam! Mosquito Heaven here & actually we wear long-sleeved shirts most of the time, Sven nothing. Pythagoras has held out manfully against Whitman with a relapse caused by the beauty of the scenery and Sven's perfect imitation of innocence. Beware angelic grins. Yr Xtn admirer Rasmus.

CONFERENCE

—These are drawings by Jeremias. That's the Life Guard, in scarlet tunic and in nothing.
—God in heaven!
—These are things we saw at the zoo. That's a bat. That, I think, is a seal.
—You bought him this expensive drawing paper?
—And crayons and watercolors.

THE GOOD CHAIR BY THE WINDOW

Inherited after a renovation of the big bedroom, the cushioned seat and back recovered in leaf brown (once paisley), with an upholstered footstool, occupancy frequently contested. Here Adam sat in sweater and briefs, heels on the seat cushion's corner edges, looking at the color plates in Pierre Chabat's *La Brique et la Terre Cuite* and answering Peter's *tell me again,* Peter being propped on pillows on the bed in yellow pyjamas, playing with himself, *all right? I orden,* and, well, Sven, who's the big tall one. I know who they are, Peter said. Sven works his dick until it gets so sensitive and great that one more slide will scud juice from his nose to his knees, and quits, timed to the second. Then, very carefully, he snugs into little gym pants, and goes and finds Rasmus, subtracts the gym pants, grits his teeth, and starts all over again with Rasmus in charge, happily, as he will have his turn next, and not coming either. When they're one tick short of being imbeciles for life, they race to the pool and swim, or run cross-country, or wallow in the snow. But mainly they keep to their crazy hugs, without their hands in each other's yellow pyjamas.

CONFERENCE

—If, Fru Overskov said, the world were any wonderfuller I couldn't stand it. Do pessimists eat rotten eggs for breakfast? But you're right: adopting Jeremias is not how he's to evolve. Adam and Peter will like the sister they're going to get.
—Yes, wonderful! Rasmus said. What would happen if I tried to adopt Jeremias?
—Do it.

AFTERNOON BIKE RIDE

Adam, Christian, and Rasmus, to the far lake beyond the lake with ducks. Willows, marshgrass, a country path to it, off the macadam road nobody uses anymore.
—A congenial wilderness, Rasmus said. A few advanced souls wander out here for philosophical picnics. I've seen Dr. Rasvinge out here with about as odd a collection of students and colleagues as you might assemble in all civilization. I remember a horn-rim-bespectacled Jap in a three-piece suit discussing some deep matter with a bronzed blonde wearing only an aptly fitted triangle of cheesecloth. We'll have to walk our bikes from here in this tall grass, to keep from running over lovers.
—O wow! Christian said. I see two girls over to the left soaking up Vitamin D all over. Pink as boiled shrimp. Teats pointing straight up.

Rasmus when he wheeled up on his bike ten minutes after calling was wearing to Adam's wonderment, and Christian's, short pants that made his legs twice as long and which in their conciseness let white segments of underwear show at the crotch when he sat. Adam's kneepants were blue, Christian's white.

A sandspit under a willow. Further along in the shallows a group of boys were wading with nets.
—Marsh zoology, Adam said. I like their outfits, one naked, one with a tank top and no bottom, two in wet underpants, and one little fellow who seems to have on everything, including shoes.
—There are two boys back of us unzipping each other.
—The godling Eros, Rasmus said, has marked this stretch of lakeside like a tomcat his territory. It's like the north end of an island Sven and I know, where the pretense of invisibility is scrupulously maintained, as there isn't much area, with lovers every square meter or so, like a medieval painting of an earthly paradise, Jack and Jill blissfully fucking over here, Tristan and Isolde over there, in an hours-long kiss, teenagers in every possible conjugation.
—Did you and Sven wrestle there, trying to kill each other because of your different, I mean, your ideas?
—One of the hundred or so leading things wrong with personal relations, Rasmus said, setting his bike on its stand, is not trusting people to love us the way we think we ought to be loved. I trust Sven, and he knows it, and he trusts me. He thinks sex is the important thing about us, and I think that love and trust are, and only when the two are in sync do I love him the way he wants to be loved. We have to swap selves to do it. Sven, you see, wants to make love to himself, and I have to become that self, as he has to become me, and then we're beautiful for awhile.
—Crazy! Christian said.
—Truly, Adam said. Is this why we're out here?
—It's an outing, on bikes, Rasmus said. Isn't that enough? I asked you along for the fun of it.
—We're not niggling, Christian said. You mussed our hair on the road and patted our behinds. Are those pants from Spejdersport?
—They're Sven's.

—Poor Sven, Christian said. You two are absolutely the most peculiar people we know.
—The friendliest, Adam said. Our pals in things we're not supposed to know about yet. We're not to stare at those boys back there, are we? They don't seem to mind who sees them.
—If we had a tadpole net we could cool our balls in the marsh.
—Mud up to your knees.

Rasmus was taking off his shoes.

—Let me explore. We are students of the green-shanked Danish moorhen, aren't we?

Rasmus waded out, sinking and lurching, right out to water up to within a few centimetres of his short pants.

—Not deep, he said, but squishy between the toes. Not for swimming, or even splashing in. Water's fresh, but awfully rich in sediment, leafmeal, and algae. How's the meditation coming along?
—We're trying, Adam said. Mama raised an eyebrow at the straw mat even though we bought it, Christian and I, made in Sri Lanka. She said more like Poland. I said we were to sit on it, in our underpants, and empty our minds. She said her hope had been for our filling them. You know mothers. I said we were going to clean our minds, which she said couldn't be done, though she approved of the effort. So Christian's on one end, I'm on the other, our hands on our knees and our feet together. There was no keeping Peter out of the room.
—I go into a trance, Christian said, and do numbers. I take five, sum of two and three, of four and one, half of and thus the little brother of ten, the system itself, one through nine with its prefacing zero shifted around to make ten, being a disguised nine all the time, no matter where it is, the number of numbers. When you collapse any number to one digit, you're always subtracting nine, though you have to do it over and over.
—I try to remember places I've been, Adam said, in particular detail, time of day, the feel of an hour last week, or the summer before. Do you know that when you and Sven were wrestling

like idiots in the pine cones, that afternoon when you sat me and Christian in each other's laps with our dinks nudging, there was a hawk that kept flying around overhead, watching?

—It was sent, Rasmus said, striding with long steps out of the marsh to lie on his back on the sandspit.

—What's hard, Christian said, is not talking. Adam and I talk all the time. He's always giving me signals about what to expect.

—We get erections, Adam said. Christian stares at my underpants.

—I get the itchies because I'm not doing anything. Mama's right when she says I can't sit still for ten minutes.

—I knew that bringing you two out for a ride would be worthwhile, Rasmus said. I could have called a girl, but she's hard to get away from, and I have reading to do, or Sven, who's harder. You are free spirits, easily pleased and full of surprises.

—Like Adam taking off his britches, as I notice.

—Not a surprise, an inevitability. The surprise would be that he kept them on.

—The boys back there on the grass, Adam said, are down in it, flat. The girls are sitting up. The zoologists have all the tadpoles they want, and are leaving.

Rasmus, laughing, stood and unbuttoned his pants, taking them off in comic haste, together with his briefs and shirt.

—To be friendly, he said.

—Water feels good, Adam said.

—Pond scum, Christian said. All yours. But I'll be friendly, too. Maybe Rasmus will put us in each other's laps again, if you wipe off the green slime.

—Come on in. Cool wet balls feel good.

Out of nowhere, from under the low branches of the willow, a boy. The most startling thing about him was his thick black eyelashes that didn't match his wild, turbulent hair, which was dark brown where it was wet, the color of straw where it was drying. He wore sopping wet dimestore underpants, sagging with genitalia more the size of Rasmus's than Christian's or

Adam's. He carried rolled dirty jeans, a dingy undershirt, and battered sneakers.

He stood, ready to run.

—Hello, Rasmus said.

The boy looked Rasmus over, and Christian, and squinted at Adam in the marsh. Rasmus noted that he needed glasses.

—I seen you up here, the boy said. I was with them, over yonder, pollywog catchers. I doubt they'll miss me. We walked out from town.

—Field trip? Rasmus asked.

—That's it, a field trip. They called it that. Are you one, too?

—We're just out biking, Christian offered, and fooling around and talking.

—That water's nasty, the boy said. Can I sort of stick here with you, if they start hollering for me, at me, like you're somebody I know and chanced on? The teacher makes out he likes me, but the pollywoggers don't, and pick on me when he's not looking. He don't like me either, but he has to act like he does.

—My name's Rasmus.

—How come you don't have on no clothes?

—And this is Christian, and that's Adam pretending he's interested in the ecology of the marsh. We're naked because we like to be. Feel welcome.

Rasmus offered a handshake. It wasn't taken.

—I could wring out my drawers, the boy said, as you're the way you are. Hang 'em out to dry on this bike, if you don't mind.

—Hypertrophy, Rasmus said under his breath.

The shaft was a rich pink tinted blue, the foreskin long and pouting, pubic hair sparse and virginal.

—Fucking awesome! Adam said.

The boy, playing his tongue along the tilt of his top lip, was trying out phrases, none of which he said.

—Adam has the manners of an honest dog, Rasmus said.

—Don't josh me, like them pollywoggers.

—Tell us your name, and we're admiring, not joshing.
—Jeremias. Now I've forgot yours.
—Christian there, Adam here, and I'm Rasmus. How old are you, Jeremias, ten?
—Twelve.
—You have beautiful eyes.

Jeremias ran a finger along his cheek, crimping the corners of his mouth.

—And you're just out here passing the time, like? On your bikes, country air, and your clothes off. I've been out here with a Life Guard I'm friends with, but if I'd told that teacher that, he'd have been all over me with Jesus.
—A Life Guard, Christian said.
—Was your dick, Mister Rasmus, as big as mine when you were twelve?
—I don't think it could have been, no.
—Oh boy!

Rasmus lay back and watched the clouds.

Jeremias suddenly quit pacing about and sat beside Christian, into whose eyes he looked.

—Do you hunt for pollywogs?
—Not so's you'd notice.
—How, Rasmus asked, as if of the sky, did you get mixed up with the field trip you're escaping from?
—Social worker made me. She's OK, a nice sort. Made me promise I'd come. Thing is, I can't get her to understand they don't want me.
—What do your parents say?

Silence. An unbelieving look from Jeremias.

—Did you bring, what's the names again, Adam and?
—Christian.
—Or them you?
—We're all friends. I asked them if they wanted to bike out here, and they jumped at it.

Jeremias thought about this, scooping up sand and letting it run through his fingers.

Adam began to say something, hushed by Christian's prodding toe.

—I'm in the way here, too, bent I?

—Not yet, Rasmus said sitting up. We're hiding you from bores and nerds, aren't we? Christian and Adam haven't made up their minds. Boys don't let their defenses down easily. You're a nice surprise. Feel welcome.

Jeremias looked even more suspicious.

—You must have took your clothes off for something.

—We like being naked, Christian said.

—You're as naked as we are, with more to show for it, Adam said.

—I wasn't going to wade in my jeans, and they said I had to wade. I got my drawers wet, and they're drying.

Home

It was the 6th of November, in the sixth year of my reign, or my captivity, which you please, that I set out on this voyage, and I found it much longer than I expected; for though the island itself was not very large, yet when I came to the east side of it, I found a great ledge of rocks lie out above two leagues into the sea, some above water, some under it, and beyond that, a shoal of sand lying dry half a league more; so that I was obliged to go a great way out to sea to double the point.

When first I discovered them, I was going to give over my enterprise, and come back again, not knowing how far it might oblige me to go out to sea; and above all, doubting how I should get back again; so I came to an anchor; for I had made me a kind of anchor with a piece of broken grappling, which I got out of the ship.

Having secured my boat, I took my gun and went on shore, climbing up upon a hill, which seemed to overlook that point, where I saw the full extent of it, and resolved to venture.

In my viewing the sea from that hill where I stood, I perceived a strong, and indeed a most furious current, which run to the east, and even came close to the point; and I took the more notice of it, because I saw there might be some danger that when I came into it, I might be carried out to sea by the strength of it and not be able to make the island again; and indeed, had I not gotten first up upon this hill, I believe it would have been so; for there was the same current on the other side the island, only that it set off at a farther distance; and I saw there was a strong eddy under the shore; so I had nothing to do but to get in out of the first current, and I should presently be in an eddy.

I lay here, however, two days; because the wind blowing pretty fresh at east-southeast, and that being just contrary to the said current, made a great breach of the sea upon the point; so that it was not safe for me to keep too close to the shore for the breach, nor to go too far off because of the stream.

The third day in the morning, the wind having abated overnight, the sea was calm, and I ventured; but I am a warning piece against all rash and ignorant pilots; for no sooner was I come to the point, when even I was not my boat's length from the shore, but I found myself in a great depth of water, and a current like the sluice of a mill. It carried my boat along with it with such violence that all I could do could not keep her so much as on the edge of it; but I found it hurried me farther and farther out from the eddy, which was on my left hand. There was no wind stirring to help me, and all I could do with my paddles signified nothing; and now I began to give myself over for lost; for as the current was on both sides of the island, I knew in a few leagues' distance they must join again, and then I was irrecoverably gone; nor did I see any possibility of avoiding it; so that I had no prospect before me but of perishing; not by the sea, for that was calm enough; but of starving for hunger. I had indeed found a tortoise on the shore, as big almost as I could lift, and tossed it into the boat, and I had a great jar of fresh water; that is to say, one of my earthen pots; but what was all this to being driven into the vast ocean, where, to be sure, there was no shore, no mainland or island for a thousand leagues at least?

And now I saw how easy it was for the Providence of God to make the most miserable condition mankind could be in worse. Now I looked back upon my desolate solitary island as the most pleasant place in the world, and all the happiness my heart could wish for was to be but there again. I stretched out my hands to it, with eager wishes. O happy desert! said I. I shall never see thee more. O miserable creature, said I, whither am I going? Then I reproached myself with my unthankful temper and how I had repined at my solitary condition; and now what would I give to be on shore again! Thus we never see the true state of our condition till it is illustrated to us by its contraries; nor know how to value what we enjoy, but by the want of it. It is scarcely possible to imagine the consternation I was now in, being driven from my beloved island (for so it appeared to me now to be) into the wide ocean almost two leagues, and in the utmost despair of ever recovering it again. However, I worked hard, till indeed my strength was almost exhausted, and kept my boat as much to the northward, that is, towards the side of the current which the eddy lay on, as possibly I could; when about noon, as the sun passed the meridian, I thought I felt a little breeze of wind in my face, springing up from the south-southeast. This cheered my heart a little and especially when, in about half an hour more, it blew a pretty small gentle gale. By this time I was gotten at a frightful distance from the island, and had the least cloud or hazy weather intervened, I had been undone another way too; for I had no compass on board, and should never have known how to have steered toward the island, if I had but once lost sight of it; but the weather continuing clear, I applied myself to get up my mast again and spread my sail, standing away to the north as much as possible, to get out of the current.

Just as I had set my mast and sail, and the boat began to stretch away, I saw even by the clearness of the water some alteration of the current was near; for where the current was so strong, the water was foul; but perceiving the water clear, I found the current abate, and presently I found to the east, at about half a mile, a breach of the sea upon some rocks; these rocks I found caused the current to part again, and as the main stress of it ran away more southerly, leaving the rocks to the northeast, so the other returned by the repulse of the rocks and made a strong eddy, which run again back to the northwest, with a very sharp stream.

They who know what it is to have a reprieve brought to them upon the ladder or to be rescued from thieves just a-going to murder them, or who have been in such like extremities, may guess what my present surprise of joy was and how gladly I put my boat into the stream of this eddy, and the wind also freshening, how gladly I spread my sail to it, running cheerfully before the wind and with a strong tide or eddy under foot.

This eddy carried me about a league in my way back again, directly towards the island, but about two leagues more to the northward than the current which carried me away at first; so that when I came near the island, I found myself open to the northern shore of it, that is to say, the other end of the island, opposite to that which I went out from.

When I had made something more than a league of way by the help of the current or eddy, I found it was spent and served me no farther. However, I found that being between the two great currents, viz., that on the south side, which had hurried me away, and that on the north, which lay about a league on the other side: I say, between these two, in the wake of the island, I found the water still and running no way, and having still a breeze of wind fair for me, I kept on steering directly for the island, though not making such fresh way as I did before.

About four o'clock in the evening, being then within about a league of the island, I found the point of the rocks which occasioned this disaster, stretching out, as is described before, to the southward, and casting off the current more southwardly, had of course made another eddy to the north, and this I found very strong, but not directly setting the way my course lay, which was due west, but almost full north. However, having a fresh gale, I stretched across this eddy, slanting northwest, and in about an hour came within about a mile of the shore, where, it being smooth water, I soon got to land.

When I was on shore, I fell on my knees, and gave God thanks for my deliverance, resolving to lay aside all thoughts of deliverance by my boat; and refreshing myself with such things as I had, I brought my boat close to the shore in a little cove I had spied under some trees and laid me down to sleep, being quite spent with the labor and fatigue of the voyage.

I was now at a great loss which way to get home with my boat. I had run so much hazard, and knew too much the case, to think of attempting it the way I went out, and what might be at the other side (I mean the west side) I knew not, nor had I any mind to run any more ventures, so I only resolved in the morning to make my way westward along the shore and see if there was no creek where I might lay my frigate in safety, so as to have her again if I wanted her; in about three miles, or there about, coasting the shore, I came to a very good inlet or bay about a mile over, which narrowed till it came to a very little rivulet or brook, where I found a very convenient harbor for my boat and where she lay as if she had been in a little dock made on purpose for her. Here I put in, and having stowed my boat very safe, I went on shore to look about me and see where I was.

I soon found that I had but a little passed by the place where I had been before, when I traveled on foot to that shore; so taking nothing out of my boat but my gun and my umbrella, for it was exceedingly hot, I began my march. The way was comfortable enough after such a voyage as I had been upon, and I reached my old bower in the evening where I found everything standing as I left it; for I always kept it in good order, being, as I said before, my country house.

I got over the fence and laid me down in the shade to rest my limbs, for I was very weary, and fell asleep. But judge you, if you can, that read my story, what a surprise I must be in, when I was waked out of my sleep by a voice calling me by my name several times, Robin, Robin, Robin Crusoe, poor Robin Crusoe! Where are you, Robin Crusoe? Where are you? Where have you been?

I was so dead asleep at first, being fatigued with rowing, or paddling, as it is called, the first part of the day and with walking the latter part that I did not wake thoroughly, but dozing between sleeping and waking, thought I dreamed that somebody spoke to me. But as the voice continued to repeat Robin Crusoe, Robin Crusoe, at last I began to wake more perfectly and was at first dreadful frighted and started up in the utmost consternation. But no sooner were my eyes open, but I saw my Poll sitting on the top of the hedge; and immediately knew that it was he that spoke to me; for just in such bemoaning language I had used to talk to him, and teach him, and he had learned it so perfectly that he would sit upon my finger and lay his bill close to my face, and cry Poor Robin Crusoe! Where are you? Where have you been? How come you here? and such things as I had taught him.

However, even though I knew it was the parrot, and that indeed it could be nobody else, it was a good while before I could compose myself. First, I was amazed how the creature got thither and then, how he should just keep about the place and nowhere else. But as I was well satisfied that it could be nobody but honest Poll, I got it over, and holding out my hand, and calling him by his name, *Poll,* the sociable creature came to me, and sat upon my thumb, as he used to do, and continued talking to me, *Poor Robin Crusoe!* and how did I come here? and where had I been? just as if he had been overjoyed to see me again; and so I carried him home along with me.

I had now had enough of rambling to sea for some time and had enough to do for many days to sit still and reflect upon the danger I had been in. I would have been very glad to have had my boat again on my side of the island; but I knew not how it was practicable to get it about. As to the east side of the island, which I had gone round, I knew well enough there was no venturing that way; my very heart would shrink and my blood run chill but to think of it. And as to the other side of the island, I did not know how it might be there; but supposing that the current ran with the same force against the shore at the east as it passed by it on the other, I might run the same risk of being driven down the stream, and carried by the island, as I had been before of being carried away from it; so with these thoughts I contented myself to be without any boat, though it had been the product of so many months' labor to make it, and of so many more to get it into the sea.

The Cardiff Team

1

If it happens that Nature, when we get up one morning and start our day, hands us exactly what we were of a mind to do, our praise comes readily, and the world looks like a meadow in the first week of creation, green, fresh, and rich in flowers.

2

An afternoon, then, of a day with so auspicious a morning. Walt and Sam, both twelve, friends who looked like brothers, at the Brasserie Georges V, Place Alma. Neat summer haircuts, white *maillots,* faded denim Andre Agassi short pants, Adidas, thick white socks crunched around their ankles, sharing a Coca. Sam picked a blade of grass from Walt's collar, grinning, nudging a foot against Walt's under the table. Walt, smug and happy, picked a fleck of leaf trash from Sam's hair. Every boy his own grin.

The waiter, who knew them as regulars with incalculable dips and rises in their means, liked their identical hair, tufts of wheat stubble with a metallic gloss, their blue eyes and burnt umber lashes.

—This Cyril we're to be tutored with at Marc's, Sam said, is he real? Sooner or later the Vincennes police will check us out, if only to run our style of sunbathing through French logic. The old gentleman walking his fat dog was on the verge of a fit, either out of curiosity or love. I'm still happy, sweet throbs and twinges.

—You're talented that way, friend Sam. Patience. The waiter is trying to figure out all over again if we're rich brats or innocents with parents in tow somewhere around the corner. He calls us *messieurs*. I like the Vincennes *bois*. Real people there. This Cyril *is* a rich brat. Daisy met his papa at some kind of do, and signalled Mama, all in about two minutes. Think of it as fun.
—I'm thinking of other things.

So they overtipped the waiter and raced each other to the apartment, with time out to admire the compliant fit of a motorcycle courier's jeans, an Alsatian on a coal barge, a concierge's tortoiseshell cat, an *agent de police* as young and handsome as Marc. Sam's Agassis followed Walt's into a chair, as a gesture toward order. Adidas, socks, *maillots*, and underpants could be picked up later by whoever still had a functioning mind.

LES GALLES

Penny and Marc at their long table, afternoon sun on stacks of books, manuscript, coffee cups.
—It's the Welsh, Penny said, he's made the painting's title, *les galles*, the Gauls from across the Sleeve. I think of the Welsh as elves singing Baptist hymns in a language as old as Latin, perhaps older. Football had come into the world, and the provincial Welsh, who hadn't been to France since Agincourt, the ones in Shakespeare, had lively rugby and soccer teams that could play in Sweden or France. Social standing has no voice in sports, or family or class. Neither is language of any matter, or religion. They got all that straight at the first Olympics, when British upper-class cyclists refused to compete with grocers' sons. Baron Coubertin put a flea in their ear. The body came into its own in a wonderful way. So here's a team of coal miners' sons playing football with the French rich, poor, and middle-class together. Their team's jerseys make them brothers in an equality hitherto unknown in the world.
—The mice who have just let themselves in down the hall, Marc

said, are, reading from left to right, Walt and Sam, one assumes, back from scandalizing the good citizens in Vincennes or Neuilly.
—With those two one assumes nothing. Just yesterday I called Walt and got Sam. So one of the things Delaunay is painting is a new kind of equality, fraternity, and decidedly liberty. Look at a kid like Calixte Delmas. whose body freed him from Lord knows what humdrum round. From ploughboy to minor divinity.
—Rousseau beat Delaunay to it, though his *footballeurs* are simply bowlers and cardplayers trying a new game.
—Rousseau beat everybody to everything.

LOG

The Cardiff Team of Robert Delaunay, begun in 1912 and finished in 1913, is a response to his friend Henri Rousseau's *The Football Players*, 1908. Delaunay's painting is resonant with a dialogue of allusions, an antiphony. Wales against England in an *agon* of rugby football. American technology in steel (the Ferris wheel) against French technology in steel (the Eiffel tower), Voisin's airplane (piloted by Henri Farman) flying in a completed circle of 771 metres vying with the Brothers Wright, who had flown at Le Mans in a figure eight when Blériot could only wobble in a straight forwardness. The radio telegraph at the top of the tower is in communication with Canada.

5

Horace, *liber quartus, carmen primum,* Sam, chin on Walt's knee and lying on the floor so that they could share a text, Marc in his nifty swivel Danish reading chair with matching footstool, Cyril over by the bookcases, everybody's idea of a rich brat. What else could you make of his designer aviator glasses, long pants, Givenchy shirt and tie?

Out Marc's windows a leafy tree and clean blue sky.
—It is, Marc said in his handsome voice, such a day as we can

imagine Horace writing this ode on his farm in the Sabine hills, with olives and pines and goats to look at. So, Cyril:

Intermissa, Venus, diu
rursus bella moves? parce precor, precor.

—Well, sir. Ablative absolute, intermission, today.
—*Diu* means now, with the sense of *after a long while.* And an intermission in a war is called a truce.
—*Rursus* is a return, so I suppose again, as *movere bella* is to declare war. I've got it, I think. After a long truce, why do you want to start a war again? Venus, goddess of love. *Parce,* in little, I pray you, I pray you.
—Give me a break, Venus, Sam said, I'm too old to be tomcatting around.
Marc laughed, in his way, and Walt knuckled Sam's head. Cyril smiled.
—Let's translate *parce* as go easy. Horace was only in his forties, but bald and running to fat.

6

Cyril consulted with the chauffeur who was waiting for him and who would not hear of his walking to the Brasserie Georges V with Walt and Sam, but would drive them there in the Rolls. He let them down on the Marceau, no hope of a parking space.
—He could have delivered us right to the curb, in front, Sam said. A taxi would have. For the edification of the waiter.
—This, Walt explained, is one of our places after an explore.
—Walt and I do long rambles, Sam said, to be together and find places and streets and whichwhat. We call them explores. Marc sometimes comes along. He's neat that way.
Cyril, as Sam remarked later, had never been among the people before, certainly not with two advanced scamps.
—Three young gentleman today, the waiter said, and what is your pleasure, *messieurs?*

—I don't have any money, Cyril whispered miserably.
—On us, Walt said. Three *picons*.
—Three Cocas! Three!

French insolence. Cyril looked appalled, Sam gave the waiter the finger to his back.

—Do you even *like* us? Sam asked, twirling a finger at Cyril. My mama, Daisy, paints these big long canvases, we'll take you and show you, with lots of figures and things, like a poster, they take months and months to do. Very realistic: she says abstractions are mud pies. Don't ever mention Francis Bacon. She takes his pictures to be a personal insult. I mean, we're stuck with each other at Marc's. Walt and I have been stuck together since we were nippers, so I know everything about him.
—Except what he's thinking and imagining, Walt said.
—Yes, but you tell me, and, besides, I know anyway.
—What Sam is grubbing for, Walt said, is how different Cyril is from us. We don't have any fathers and he doesn't, he says, at the moment have a maman. He lives out near the Bagatelle, and we live *centre ville*. We, I think, have more liberty and equality, which leaves fraternity, which is what we're going for.
—Say you like us, Sam said
—Yes, Cyril said.
—Add *so far*, Walt said. Liking somebody is really liking what they like, to share. Sam and I don't know a lot of kids, as we're different, in our way, and scare people off.

Cyril looked troubled.

—Marc says we're not to scare you off, but make friends.
—Whales, Sam said, is what busses are, of two plunging toward the bridge.

Walt tilted his chair back, shoved his hands into his pockets, and beamed.

—Let's make friends, he said. Sniff each other like good dogs. You're Cyril. We're Walt and Sam. Marc is finishing us before *les vacances*. Stuffing us with culture.
—Babysitting us, Sam said.

—Marc is Maman's assistant sort of, and Sam's mother is mine's best friend. Maman's other best friend I suppose you could say Marc is.
—What do they do, Cyril asked, Monsieur Bordeaux and your mother?
—Well, Sam said, answering for Walt, whose mouth was full, they read books together and make notes and discuss things. Last week, for instance, they were reading Spengler paragraph by paragraph, and talking about it and making notes. Something about epoch and style. They sit very close. Penny sticks her fingers in Marc's hair and he kisses the back of her neck. Marc types things up for her, and fetches books, and looks things up in libraries. Toward the end of the afternoon they fuck. If they make a baby, Walt and I are going to change its diapers, salt it with talcum, and take it on our explores.
—What is Spengler? Cyril asked.
—A totally bald German who wrote a big book about how everything has a style.

Walt with a minim of eyeshift gave Sam the long boy at the *cabine téléphone* on the corner whose only garment was flimsy kneepants so low on his hips his wallet hung on its fold in back dragged them down to his butt. Tummy plank flat. Dirty bare feet.
—Noted, Sam nodded. Gauze pyjama bottoms and no underpants. Catch the dumb girl from Atlanta on the terrace, ordering whiskey.
—It's our anthropology, Walt said to Cyril. Sometimes we interact with subject, but mainly we just watch and swap comments, though we usually know what the other's thinking. Yesterday we walked a three-piece suit and bowler against a lamppost by kissing and grabbing each other by the crotch.

Cyril's nubble nose twitched, his big gray eyes became as round as francs, and his mouth squeezed into a lopsided smile.
—Why? he asked.

—To get even. A three-piece suit and bowler conked by a lamppost is a score.
—I meant, Cyril said, swallowing hard, grabbing.
—Oh we're always doing that. Keeps us happy.
—Actually, Sam said, we're reasonably civilized, being groomed to take our place, as Maman says, in the aristocracy of adolescence that has ruled France since the Third Republic. So, along with Marc's seminar for twelve-year-old geniuses, which, who knows, may someday be as famous as Alexandre Kojève's, we're into urban anthropology, anarchy, and sex.
—Sex, Cyril said, looking into his empty glass. I'll be twelve in a month and two days.
—Your keeper, Walt said, is looking meaningfully this way. Look, tell him we're going on an explore. Better still, send him home.

Cyril took a deep breath, looked grim, and said he'd try.
—Golly, Sam said. Stuck with a nursemaid whose perambulator is a Rolls. They seem to be making a deal. What Cyril wants to do is trade off free time with us for whatever the chauffeur wants to sneak into his day, belote at the bistro, an afternoon fuck, or fishing from the quays.
—If Cyril has any rascal in him, which we're doubting.
—He has. Monsieur le Chauffeur is furious.

The Rolls would follow them at a discreet distance. They were to stay in sight of it.
—That's what he thinks, Sam said.
—He said he'd lose his job.

On the explore, which began with crossing the Pont d'Alma, Cyril learned that Sam's mother is a painter and that Walt's writes about painting and philosophy and whichwhat, that sex is a kind of secret game and lots of fun, that Walt's mama, with Marc as her research assistant, is writing a study of Robert Delaunay's *The Cardiff Team,* that iconography is the study of things in paintings, that Robert Delaunay was a painter scads of years ago, that Sam's mother had a neat friend named Christofer, a Norwegian who doesn't speak French too good but is seven feet tall, is hung like a horse, and is handsome, that they all had the use of a house in the country, on weekends, where you run naked in the orchard, that if you go to the Grande Jatte Island it's all built over with houses and not at all like Seurat's painting, that all Russians are hysterical, that Penny and Daisy had been to Denmark to see all of the paintings there of one Vilhelm Hammershøj, that Walt and Sam sleep together at his place when Christofer is spending the night at Daisy's, as Christofer is a Lutheran and shy, that Sam and Walt had read almost all of Jules Verne, that Penny was reading them a neat book called *King Matt the First* as a bedtime book, that flowers and trees and weeds have names which Sam and Walt knew and he didn't, that somebody named Lévi-Strauss had left licorice out of a list of aromas and that somebody named Fourier hadn't, that the ancient Greeks loved boys and girls, that Penny, Daisy, and Marc owned no automobile nor television set; that Sam and his mother live in a studio on the Boulevard Berthier; that Germany is an entire nation of white trash; that both Sam and Walt are bastards; that there is a film and recording of the poet Apollinaire; that for reasons grinned at but not explained, Sam and Walt have been to one school or another, never for long, and have mainly been taught by their mothers, with occasional tutors like Marc; that there was once a woman tutor who quit in high dudgeon after a week; that Sam and Walt seemed to have endless conversations with their mothers; and that he was a very lonely little boy.

Sam and Walt learned far more than Cyril was aware of telling them.

7

Cyril's papa's secretary had called back. Yes, Cyril could go to Saint-Germain-en-Laye with the seminar. It was much preferred that the chauffeur drive them all out, but if Monsieur Bordeaux chooses to go by train, that is acceptable. It was hoped that Cyril would not get too warm on a walk in the historic forest, or too fatigued in the museum.

—Cyril's being decanted from the Rolls, Sam said at Marc's window. He's wearing a suit, with tie.

—Hallo, Cyril, Marc said. Sam and Walt, hanging out the window to admire the Rolls, have had a good idea, I really should have told you that we'll be tramping about in the forest, as well as the big museum. Walt keeps togs here, and will gladly lend you kneepants like his and Sam's, and even sneakers.

—Here, Walt said, laundry fresh and all. Off your high-mass capitalist uniform.

Cyril, worried, stood fixed in indecision.

—Here, Sam said, bringing a coat hanger. We'll be, you see, a team, all dressed alike.

—I keep a change of clothes here, Walt said. Actually, we can all have yellow polo shirts. Sneakers won''t quite be the same, but white sweatsocks will make up for that.

—Change clothes *here?* Cyril asked.

—We're all boys together, Marc said. No reason to be shy. Sam and Walt have never heard of modesty.

There were cuts of eye from Walt to Sam when Cyril, blushing, stood in underpants that came up to his ribcage.

—You won't need an undervest with Walt's shirt, Marc said. It's a warm day.

—The pants fit good, Walt said. Sam and I wear each other's clothes so much we don't know which is which any more, and our mothers have given up trying. Anyway, when Maman buys me anything, she gets two of 'em, one for Sam too, and Daisy, Sam's maman, does the same.

—Is this OK with you, Cyril? Marc asked. I like my three mice looking, at a glance, at least, like triplets.

—Yes, Cyril said, with a smile. It feels funny, but I think I like it.

—Practical, shall we say, and they're becoming.

8

Crossing the road in Saint-Germain-en Laye, Marc took Cyril's hand, as a matter of course. Sam and Walt had held hands, off and on, all day. It was their style. Cyril's hand was awkward to hold, and when Sam, earlier, put an arm across Cyril's shoulders, he had flinched and stiffened. Walt had exchanged glances with Marc.

Lunch at outdoor tables in the English Garden. Ham and cheese sandwiches, a beer for Marc, which Walt sipped from, Coca Colas for Sam and Cyril.

—I liked hearing about l'Abbé Breuil and Teilhard Chardin, Cyril said, and James II of England and General Leclerc. Will we, M. Bordeaux, see the rest of the museum, the medieval part and the Celtic?

—Oh for gosh sakes, Walt said. Call Marc Marc.

—Yes, Marc said, but not today. You've learned enough for one morning. Who wants apple tart, all of us? Do you take coffee, Cyril? And I'd like it if you call me Marc.

—I don't think so. I mean, though, if everybody is, I will too.

—Walt hates coffee, Marc said, but he drinks it because I do, and suspects that it will put hair on his chest and make his voice change faster and make his peter grow. Sam, who's honest, will have milk. I'm bringing two coffees and two milks. Nobody needs to prove anything by drinking coffee.

—I like it, Sam said, when Marc turns into a nursemaid. God help his children.

—Do you know the forest here, Cyril? Walt asked.

—No. My parents have some friends here, and I've driven through, but I've never been around on foot, like today, or to the museum.

—The forest is big. I may climb a tree. All the animals are gone.

Marc returned with a waiter bringing four apple tarts and two boxes of milk. He himself brought two coffees. They made their way around a family of Americans, bald the father, blue-haired the mother, and two daughters who kept fussing with their long hair. They were taking the table across the gravel walk, looking all about them,

Walt and Sam turned to each other, embraced, and kissed.

—It's a game, Marc said to Cyril. To make the Americans nervous. Join in, if you want to. I'm used to it.

Cyril arranged a kind of smile.

—Eat up, before the waiter asks us to leave.

—You think? Walt said, standing to lean and kiss Marc on the corner of the mouth. We haven't even petted each other's dinks yet.

—Cyril, Marc said, putting his arm around him and talking close to his ear, we can't pretend we don't know these urchins, and our civilized unconcern will be part of the theatre, OK? If one of them kisses you, kiss back. They're joshing the Americans, not us.

Cyril slid his arm around Marc's shoulder, weightless but nevertheless there.

—Cyril's learning, Sam said brightly.

KRZYZANOWSKI

—The Eiffel Tower, Penny read, a quadruped giant who held his steel head high above the traffic, chatter, and music of Paris, high enough, you understand, to put up with the noises of the crowd below, the busy streets, the bang and clamor, the shouts. And it was these crazy people milling about his feet who had installed in his head that rose into the clouds the radio station that received signals from all over the world. And if someone named Walter thinks I didn't see him sneak off his pyjama pants and stuff them under the bolster before he got into bed he has porridge for brains.

—Interpol should be staffed with nothing but mothers, Walt said. All the crooks would be caught within minutes.

—Vibrations from space having chimed in his brain that bristled so high in the air, they then flowed down his interlaced muscles of steel, and sank through his feet into the ground, The tower shook itself, shifting from foot to foot. It heaved, pulled its toes from the earth, and quivered from top to bottom.

—Who wrote this? Sam asked. My pyjama bottoms are on, though somebody has his hand inside them.

—Sigismund Dominikovitch Krzyzanowski. It was, all this, just at dawn, when everybody was still asleep under the shelter of their roofs, when the Place des Invalides, the Champs de Mars, the streets roundabout, and the quays, are empty and quiet. The three-hundred-meter-tall giant wiggled the numb and cold out of his ponderous feet, and, hammering flat the steel curve of a bridge and twisting awry the stone steps of the Trocadero, took the rue d'Iena toward the Bois de Boulogne.

—King Kong! Walt said. Godzilla.

—But this was written in, let's see, 1927. Feeling hemmed in by streets, bumping against buildings, the Eiffel Tower kicked sleeping apartment houses out of his way. They collapsed like cardboard boxes. Less frightened than embarrassed by his clumsiness, for the houses were joined to each other, and when one went down, others followed, he stomped along, crunch crunch. Meanwhile, Paris awoke: searchlights pierced the morning fog, fire sirens honked, and buzzing airplanes rose into the air. Whereupon, the Tower raised his elephant's feet and began to make haste over roofs, which crashed down with every step. He has reached the edge of the Bois, cutting a swath through it with his steel knees.

—Ha Ha! Walt said, getting his nose pinched by Sam.

—The day began bright and sunny. Three million Parisians awoke to the noise, and panicked. They fled to the train stations. Newspaper presses began to roll, with enormous headlines about the wandering Tower, and telephones passed on the catastrophe. In full daylight Parisians could see the empty space where, every morning before, they had, by habit, looked at the Tower. Witnesses reported seeing the giant wading the Seine, others saw it jumping over Montmartre, but with the clearing of the morning fog, most of these rumors proved false. Three million irate citizens were in despair, enraged, flinging accusations and demanding the return of the fugitive Tower. American tourists in the hotels around the Place Monceau ran out with their kodaks and photographed the mammoth footprints, the dead, and the ruins. A poet (on foot for economy's sake) who had walked from Saint-Celestin, nibbled his pencil at the edge of an enormous footprint, and with a pensive air began a moralizing poem about it all.

—Is this for real? Sam asked.

—The poet was in a quandary as to whether the subject called for alexandrines or the meanderings of free verse. And the Tower, quivering to keep its balance, stomped ever onward. It sank into soft earth at every step, and if it knew very well where it had come from, it had only the vaguest idea where it was going. Chance took it to the northwest, toward the coast. It wanted to find a road, and what then? Suddenly it ran into a semicircle of artillery, which it smashed, and turned north. It was stopped by the ramparts of Anvers, with cannon. Shells bounced against the tower. Blindly, its joints loosened, it fled to the southeast, and longed to return to the place where it had been put by its creators. But then it heard, almost as a whisper, in its radio brain: *Along this way!*

—That's neat, Walt said. The radio station on top is its brain.

—You and I, O Reader, know whence the message came.

—We do? Sam asked.

—This is a Russian story, Penny said. Now the Tower knew where to go. It headed east. He had liberated himself; he would join others who had done the same. Agitated telegraph wires clicked from capital to capital: The enraged monster has become a Bolshevik! Stop him! Infamy! Spare no effort! We must join forces! Again the path of the fleeing Tower is blocked by artillery. Again, in a barrage of steel against steel, the colossal quadruped sings in its metallic voice a savage and terrible song. Wounded, riddled with shell bursts, his bristling head trembling, he stalks on, nearer and nearer to the summons from the Revolution. Already he imagines he can see red flags like poppies in a vast prairie, thick columns of people rank upon rank. He imagines a loud square enclosed by an ancient crenelated wall. That is where he will place his iron *sabots.* Kicked aside, armies retreat and open his way. The diplomats think furiously in storms of thought: He has escaped, has slipped through our lines. We must take extraordinary measures, but what can we do? Shall I stop here?

—Don't you dare! Sam said.

—So it was that the metal giant's pursuers, half crushed by his feet of steel, moved their battles into the air. The antennae of Paris, New York, Berlin, Chicago, London, Rome found the frequency, often a mere whisper: *This way! This way!* They made promises, sang and seduced, jamming the transmissions from the east. The monster became confused. It lost its way. It began to move south, and then staggered about like a blind man. The radio signals were a whirlwind of noise, driving him crazy and depleting his strength. There was rejoicing in the capitals, hands clapped with joy. Villages and towns between the wandering Tower and Paris were evacuated. Around the church of the Invalides and the Champ de Mars preparations were made for the Tower's return, defeated and chastened, but with a ceremonial welcome. But on its way back, where three frontiers meet, it came to a sheet of water squeezed between mountain peaks: the serene and deep Lake Constance. Passing around it, the vanquished giant saw in its blue mirror his own reflection upside down and strewn with flecks of sunlight, extending from the shore to the middle of the lake, its tip sunk into the depths. A shiver of sonorous disgust shook the Tower—in a final paroxysm of rage, as if breaking invisible bonds, it raises its ponderous feet, rears up, and from the high alpine terraces (just imagine!), plunges in headfirst. Behind it crashed an avalanche of loosened rock and broken boulders, and then, from one mountain pass to another, the echo of sundered water splashing over all of the

lakeshore. The steel feet of the suicide, after a dying spasm, fixed in the rigor of death.
—That's it? Walt asked.
—Well, it's a story inside another story. The writer is reading it to fellow authors, one of whom objects that Lake Constance is ninety kilometers long and would scarcely overflow because three hundred meters of openwork steel fell into it; and another points out that towers do not customarily walk anywhere.
Sam looked at Walt, Walt at Sam.

L'EQUIPE DE CARDIFF

Sam, Walt, Cyril in the Museum of Modern Art of the City of Paris.
—This is it, Walt said. The box-kite aeroplane is Henri Farman's, pioneer aviator. We can show you his grave in Chaillot, with a bas-relief of him piloting his stick-and-canvas flying machine, a Voisin pusher biplane. He invented ailerons. The Wright brothers had to twist their wings by pulling on a cord. He and his brother Maurice manufactured aircraft and had the first airline between London and Paris. The English poet who wrote *A Shropshire Lad,* Alfred Housman, who was a professor of Greek at Cambridge, used to grade his students' *bachots* at the end of term and take the Farman Goliath for Paris, as he liked taxi drivers, which he couldn't do in England, as they're Protestants.
—Why did he like taxi drivers? Cyril asked.
—The big red wheel is *la grande roue de Ferris,* the American engineer. You ride on it in seats, which roll you up and over, over and down, making your insides turn upside down sideways. The three billboards: the one on the left is a word ending in AL, and Penny hasn't found out yet what it is, and ASTRA is a company that made aeroplanes, and then DELAUNAY, which is both Robert's signature and Sonia's too, as she illustrated a book by Blaise Cendrars, who had one arm, and wrote a poem about New York. He traveled all over, Siberia and Panama, and caught

monkeys and parrots for zoos. And then the football players. Penny is working on their pants and jerseys, socks and shoes, their evolution of design. Everything in the painting had just come into the world.

11

Marc cracked Walt's door at dawn, whistling three notes.
—Marc? Walt whispered, one eye open. What's up?
—A swim before breakfast, Tiger. Jeans, sneakers, and a sweater's all you need. I'll give you three minutes.
—Holy cow!
—One.
—You really mean it?
—Two.

A naked Walt tiptoed out, jeans snatched from a chair in one hand, sneakers and socks scooped from the floor in the other. Marc sent him back for a sweater, bottom drawer.
—Penny's asleep, Marc whispered. Way down.
—So's Bee, a bubble of spit on her lips. I have to piss.
—At the gym, five minutes.
—I need briefs. And a *slip?*
—None of the above. You can put your sneakers on downstairs.

Out on the boulevard, zipping up his fly, smoothing his hand around his face, Walt ran to catch up with Marc, skipping to keep pace.

Club Sportif Hermès. Marc had a key to it on a fine gold chain around his neck. Carpeted lounge walled by milky glass. Bright lights down a corridor, a long pool with clear green water, cold to smell. A *bonjour* from bejind a row of lockers, and then a tall acorn-brown boy with copper hair, wearing only an oatmeal-gray sweatshirt.
—Talk about early, he yawned.
—Pissoirs are in through there, Marc said to Walt, who was beginning to dance. I see I've beat the general.

—Almost beat me. If you have two girls, one's sure to find out about the other sooner or later, wouldn't you say? As in the films.
—Two girls! Walt said. Hello, I'm Walt.
—Jean-Luc, smiled the attendant. At this time of morning I cannot worry that you are very obviously not fifteen.
—He's getting there, Marc said. He's family. I spent the night with his mother, and he spent the night with his mother's best friend's daughter, his age.
—*Mon Dieu!* said Jean-Luc. And I hear the general.

Marc slotted cleanly into the pool from the short diving board, followed by Walt, who bobbed up like a pert seal in his wake, frogging along with a breaststroke. They met at the far end, and shoulder to shoulder pushed off together, Marc slowing his crawl to be friendly.
—Four lengths, he said.
—As many as you say, Walt gasped.
—Four lengths.

The old general was emerging pink and sagging from a complexity of trousers, suspenders, and long underwear, helped by Jean-Luc, when Marc and Walt heaved themselves onto the pool's edge, barely winded.
—Cold?
—Naw. Feels good.
—The general over there's eighty if he's a day.
—His balls hang down like a billy goat's.

Walt when he was happy babbled. Marc's balls, he observed in a discreet voice, were tight and plump, like his. The old general seemed to like Jean-Luc, who *was* good-looking, yes?

The general splatted into the pool in a geysering splash and Jean-Luc hit himself in the forehead with a fist and palmed his genitals.
—Maman says I'm polymorphously perverse, or polyversely permorphous, which is why Bee dresses as a boy who might be my brother or best friend named Sam.

—Which you do for a hoot. Penny also said, I mean to me, that I should be pals with you, not so much as a father, I'm a bit young for that, as a big brother. Two boys, and Bee as Sam, can tangle and monkey with each other without undue attention from the public.

—You're eighteen. That's old.

—Not up there, though, with the general. Who seems to be drowning.

—Jean-Luc is looking as if it isn't his day.

—So what do you think, do I get to play big brother?

—Do you like me?

—Oh no. You're a pukey brat who's doing God knows what at twelve with his smart lovely mother's full approval, who has some phenomenal IQ, is charming, and so, I'm informed, jacks off while studying Dutch publications illustrated with Dutch boys who began by jiggling it in their diapers and are now into advanced states of happy idiocy.

Walt frowned.

—Penny wasn't snitching. Information, rather, to wise me up as a friendly big brother.

Walt kicked his heels in the pool. Jean-Luc was helping the wheezing general out, two big towels draped around his neck.

—When I think I'm ahead of Maman, I usually find out I'm behind. Bee, too? You'd get the two of us, wouldn't you?

—Better and better.

—I think I'm confused. Confused good, not bad confused.

—We'll make it up as we go along. This swim was a start. Do things with him, Penny said. So I thought I'd bring you to my workout place for a skinny swim while the girls are still asleep, or maybe awake and comparing notes.

—You think?

—Girls are girls.

12

At the Grand Corona, at tables on the *trottoir*, Sam and Walt in new Norwegian blue kneepants, mustard pullovers, thick white sweatsocks and sneakers. Penny, Daisy, and Marc.
—We like the togs, Sam said, putting an arm around Walt's shoulders.
—I've overheard two *what charming boys* so far, in the museum, and one *are they twins?* and a distinguished gentleman breathing hard when the imps had a hand in each other's back pocket rather more affectionately than he was used to seeing.
—We stumbled another by stealing a kiss on the stairs.
—There's a woman in the Parc Floral still trying to figure out why Sam went with Daisy to the *Femmes* and I went alone to the *Hommes.* And in the *Hommes* was a wee tyke who had dropped his ice cream inside his shirt and by the time his maman got him to the wash basins, inside his pants too. *She* was in the wrong place. Was it his maleness, negligible as it was, that made her take him there to rinse him and his rompers?
—Structuralism, Daisy sighed, structuralism.

13

In front of the Champ de Mars, the Eiffel Tower, placed upon its four iron pillars, forms the Arch of Triumph of Science and Industry.

Its aspect, now that it is finished to its definite height, can be judged of and appreciated. Its early detractors are mute, and the approbation of engineers and artists is unanimous. When regarded from a distance, the 300-meter tower appears graceful, slender, and light. It rises toward the heavens like a delicate latticework of wires, and, as a whole, it is all full of poesy. When it is approached, the structure becomes monumental, and when the base of the colossus is reached, the spectator gazes with admiration and meditation at this enormous mass, assembled with mathematical precision, and forming one of the boldest works that the art of the engineer has ever dared to undertake. This surprise increases when he ascends the staircase of the tower. Before reaching the first story, he traverses forests of iron uprights, which offer fantastic entanglements; then, in measure as he ascends, he is astonished at once at the immensity of the structure, its apparent lightness, and the splendor of the panorama that it permits of contemplating. Apart from the undoubted interest that attaches to the Eiffel Tower, as much from the standpoint of its metallic structure as from that of its height, we can now no longer deny that the gigantic work is absolutely beautiful.

Sunday, March 31, 1889, while descending the tower stairs after the ceremony of placing the flag upon the summit, we had the pleasure of hearing one of our most distinguished members of the Academy of Science exclaim that this iron monument was certainly the most astonishing production of our age. It is for our epoch, he said to us, what the Great Pyramid, which interprets the efforts of an entire people, was for the ancient world. All the resources of contemporary art have had to concur in its execution. The work that M. Eiffel will have had the glory of carrying out is, in fact, the expression of the applied science of our time.

VERBASCUM THAPSUS LINNAEUS

Champ de Mars, promenade with benches, flower beds by Caillebotte, sky by Rousseau, with *montgolfier* and vapor trails.
—Like this, Walt said, standing toe to toe with Sam. Friendly space, see, and how friendly can you be? I lean in, and Sam leans in, not touching, not yet, knees as close as can be, front of our pants, chin, nose. Fingertips together. It worries people a lot.
—Can three do it? Cyril asked.
—In a bit. We have to be looking deep into each other's eyes, like ow, before we start wandering hands. That has to be real sneaky.

—Pretend you're not with us, Sam said. Sit on the bench there and think about algebra or something.
—You look like you're daring each other to fight.
—It's foreplay, sort of, Walt said.

15

Sam, interested, watched at Marc's window until the Rolls decanted Cyril.
—He's getting out before the chauffeur can open the door for him. A blow for democracy. Nor is he wearing a tie.
Sam and Walt looked at each other. Marc went to the door.
—Hullo everybody, Cyril said, wriggling out of his jacket. I still have Sam's pants, maybe Walt's, from the country, so all I need is somebody's jersey, and can I be barefoot?
—Why do you think you need to ask? Walt said, following Cyril into the bedroom.
—Golly, Sam said, barefoot. Fall of the Bastille. The women of Paris march to Versailles.
—This calls for hot chocolate, wouldn't you say? Marc asked Sam. Do you know how to heat milk, slowly, so that it does't scorch? I was going to take us all to the Musée de l'Homme, to learn about Leroi Gourhan.
—Esquimaux, Sam said, Les Combarelles, Les Éyzies de Tayac.
—Walt and I, Cyril said, have kissed on the corners of the mouth.
—And now Cyril and Sam, Sam said, with a hug. And Marc, whose after-shave is spiffy.
—We also, Walt said, kissed one or two other things, to be friendly, owing to their being available while changing, for the revolutionary note.
—Never let an opportunity go to waste, Marc said, setting out four mugs and a box of sugar. Let's all hug, me and Cyril, Cyril and Sam, Sam and me, and on around. The milk! Revolutionary affection and making chocolate is a tricky business. But before

this round of mutual esteem proceeds to sucking toes, whoofing in ears, licking navels, and rubbing noses, let's sit down to our chocolate and start learning some ethnography.
—Sucking toes? Cyril said.
—Let's do all those things when we get back, Walt said. I saw some coconut vanilla biscuits in the cupboard.

THE FIELD PATH: HEDGEROW WITH FINCHES

Owls are the moths of birds.

Cobwebs and rabbit by Rimbaud. Ladybird on hawthorn leaf. A startled bird the flight of an arrow from the bow of Eros, and is there another pun in Heraclite: the bow is both life and death: the bow is sometimes that of Eros, that of Ares? Eros and the curve of time.

> Watch the knowing owl with open wings
> Who has flown from Athena's shoulder
> On Olympos, and lights in this tree.
>
> The swan's grace he lacks, but his quick
> Yellow eye can read the book of the dark,
> Can read the deep of the night's silence.

Nietzsche: The superfluous is the enemy of the necessary.

17

Walt sat in Marc's kitchen studying the *café filtre,* looking into the lid of the canister, listening to the drip.

Scorched chicory and roasted chestnuts.
—The better bistros had them years ago, Marc said, before everything changed, before my time, way before yours.

They had met, as arranged, in the park, where they jogged. Marc's onionskin running shorts were transparent enough for the deep pouch and blue oval trademark of his jockstrap to show through. Barefoot, hairy toes. Good for the feet, he said. Walt in denim kneepants, white tank top, sandals, and tall blue socks, had come to watch, but after Marc had run ten laps around the parterre, shiny with sweat, he easily cajoled Walt into joining him.

—I'll never keep up.

—I'll trot.

So Walt had run barefoot, too, and like an elf, weightless. Hermes and Eros.

—I'd thought jogging was for grown-ups, but I like it, you know? Except I think I ruined my feet.

Marc's apartment was in Walt's opinion neat, spiffy, and great. And neat Perrier water supercold from the fridge, and spiffy the *café filtre* dripping through, and great that they'd had a shower, not quite together, as there wasn't room, but as good as. Marc got the water right, and Walt went first, and when he was soaped up and grinning, Marc changed the water to ice cold and explained how to enjoy it while he turned blue and broke out in goose bumps.

THE GREAT WHEEL AT CHICAGO

The wonderful *merry-go-round* designed by Engineer George W. G. Ferris, of Pittsburgh, Pa., is now completed and forms a most remarkable and attractive object. This curious piece of mechanism carries thirty-six pendulum cars, each seating forty passengers; thus one revolution of the wheel carries 1,440 people to a height of 250 feet in the air, giving to each passenger a magnificent view and a sensation of elevation akin to that of a balloon ascent. The practical working of the great machine is attended with perfect success, and its construction and operation reflect the highest credit on the author.

The description of the construction of the great wheel given in the Chicago *Tribune* will be of interest: The wheel is composed of two wheels of the same size, connected and held together with rods and struts, which, however, do not approach closer than twenty feet to the periphery. Each wheel has for its outline a curved, hollow, square iron beam, 25½ x 19 inches. At a distance of fourty feet within this circle is another circle of a lighter beam. These beams are called crowns, and are connected and held together by an elaborate trusswork. Within this smaller circle there are no beams, and at a distance there appears to be nothing.

But at the center of the great wheel is an immense iron axle, 32 inches thick and 45 feet in length. Each of the twin wheels, where the axle passes through it, is provided with a large iron hub, 16 feet in diameter. Between these hubs and the inner crowns there are no connections except spoke rods, 2½ inches in diameter, arranged in pairs, 13 feet apart at the crown connection. At a distance they look like mere spider webs, and the wheel seems to be dangerously devoid of substantial support.

The explanation of this is that the Ferris wheel—at least inside the smaller crowns—is constituted on the principle of a bicycle wheel. The lower half is suspended from the axle by the spoke rods running downward, and the upper half of the wheel is supported by the lower half. All the spoke rods running from the axle north, when it is in any given position, might be removed, and the wheel would be as solid as it would be with them. The only difference is that the Ferris wheel hangs by its axle, while a bicycle wheel rests on the ground, and the weight is applied downward on the axle.

The thirty-six carriages of the great wheel are hung on its periphery at equal intervals. Each car is twenty-seven feet long, thirteen feet wide, and nine feet high. It has a heavy frame of iron, but is covered externally with wood. It has a door and five broad plate glass windows on each side. It contains forty revolving chairs, made of wire and screwed to the floor. It weighs thirteen tons, and with its forty passengers will weigh three tons more. It is suspended from the periphery of the wheel by an iron axle six and one-half inches in diameter, which runs through the roof. It is provided with a conductor to open the doors, preserve order, and give information. To avoid accidents from panics and to prevent insane people from jumping out, the windows will be covered with an iron grating.

It is being considered whether each car shall not have a telephone connection with the office on the ground. It is thought that this would be an attraction, both as a sort of amusement for people who wish to converse with their friends below or in another car and as a sort of reassurance to timid people. The thought of being detained up in the clouds, as it were, by accident, and not being able to learn what it is or when it will be remedied, might frighten some timid people out of making the trip. It is not very difficult, however, to climb by the wheel itself to any car, and there will always be men on the ground who can do this.

The wheel, with its cars and passengers, weighs about 1,200 tons, and therefore needs something substantial to hold it up. Its axis is supported, therefore, on two skeleton iron towers, pyramidal in form, one at each end of it. They are 40 x 50 feet at the bottom and 6 feet square at the top, and about 140 feet high, the side next to the wheel being perpendicular, and the other sides slanting. Each tower has four great feet, and each foot rests on an underground concrete foundation 20 x 20 x 20 feet. Crossbars of steel are laid at the bottom of the concrete, and the feet of the tower are connected with and bolted to them with iron rods.

One would naturally suppose that there would be great danger of making such a huge wheel as this lopsided or untrue, so that it would not revolve uniformly. Even if the wheel itself were perfectly true, it would seem that the unequal distribution of passengers might make it eccentric in its speed. But according to L. V. Rice, the superintendent of construction, there is absolutely no danger of this kind. Not only did the wheel alone turn uniformly, but when the cars were hung, one after another, no inequality was observed. As to passengers, Mr Rice says that the

1,400 passengers will have no more effect on the movement of the speed than if they were so many flies.

The wheel, however, is never left to itself, but is always and directly and constantly controlled by a steam engine. The wheel points east and west, and the one-thousand horsepower reversible engine which runs it is located under the east half of it and sunk four feet in the ground. The machinery is very similar to that used in the power houses of the cable-car companies, and runs with the same hoarse roar that they do. It operates a north-and-south iron shaft 12 inches in diameter, with great cog-wheels at each end, by means of which the power is applied at each side of the wheel.

The periphery of both of the great outer crowns of the great wheel is cogged, the cogs being about six inches deep and about eighteen inches apart, and the power of the engine is applied at the bottom of the wheel. Underneath the wheel, in line with the crowns on each side, are two sprocket wheels nine feet in diameter, with their centers sixteen feet apart. They are connected by an immense endless driving chain, which plays on their own cogs and on the cogs of the great wheel as well. These sprocket wheels are operated by the engine at the will of the engineer, who can turn the wheel either way, and fast or slowly, as he may wish. The wheel is 250 feet in diameter, 825 feet in circumference, and 30 feet wide, and is elevated 15 feet above the ground.

The great wheel is also provided with brakes. Near the north and south ends of the main shaft are two ten-feet wheels, with smooth faces, and girdled with steel bands. These bands terminate a little to one side in a large Westinghouse air brake. If therefore anything should break, and the engine fail to work, the air can be turned into the air brake, and the steel band tightened until not a wheel in the whole machine can turn. In the construction of this great wheel every conceivable danger has been calculated and provided for. Windage was a matter of the greatest importance, for, although the wheel itself is all open work, the cars present an immense resisting surface. But Mr Rice points to the two towers, with their bases fifty feet north and south of the wheel, and bolted into twenty feet of concrete, and says that a gale of a 100 miles an hour would have no effect. He says that all the frost and snow that should adhere to the wheel in winter would not affect it; and that if struck by lightning it would absorb and dissipate the thunderbolt so that it would not be felt.

It is arranged to empty and refill six cars with passengers at a time, so that there will be stops in every revolution. Accordingly six railed platforms, of varying heights, have been provided on the north side of the wheel, and six more, corresponding with these, on the south side of it. When the wheel stops, each of the six lowest cars will have a platform at each of its doors. Then the next six cars will be served the same way, and the next and the next all day, and perhaps all night. It is expected that the wheel will revolve once only in every twenty minutes. Passengers will remain on board during two revolutions and pay fifty cents for their fun.

The Ferris Wheel Company was capitalized at $600,000, and $300,000 worth of bonds were issued and sold. The final concession for the erection of the wheel was not granted until December, and all the work has been contracted for and done since then, the iron having been in the pig in January, while the scaffolding was not begun until March 20. By the terms of the concession, the company pays to the Exposition one-half of all its receipts after they have amounted to the cost of the wheel. On the day the wheel was first started, June 21, 1893, five thousand guests were present at the inaugural ceremonies, all of whom were given a ride on the great wheel. The motion of the machinery is said to have been almost imperceptible.

19

Cyril was in a raincoat, Junior London Fog, with hat and umbrella. Galoshes.

—Going to the North Pole? Walt asked. You've just made Father Adam be civilized, as he says.
—I did? Cyril smiled. I've had breakfast. Told a big fib about when I'm to be here.
—Got to sniff your raincoat, Walt said. You smell like a department store. Get out of all those counterrevolutionary habiliments and slurp coffee with us.
—If Walt wants to look at my dick with big solemn eyes, Marc said, who am I to deny the simpleminded?
—Walt! Cyril said from the bedroom, where are your underpants? I get to wear them, right?
—We couldn't find 'em this morning. Marc said they're on the stairs outside. Look around the bed. I'm putting two sugars in your coffee. Skip underpants.
—If, Marc said after a swallow of coffee, the god Eros, smelling of wild thyme and meadow dill between his toes, curls rumpled by his mother's hands, legs bronzed by Arcadian light, his fingers smelling of the goat and olive aroma of his pert little spout, his pagan eyes busy with mischief, his balls as tight and tender as a fat fig, his dimples set deep with his power over cock and hen, bee and flower, bull and cow, is still frisky, there's no cause for bashfulness. Or.
—Say it again, Walt said, I'll write it down.
—Is it a poem? Cyril asked.
—Or, Marc went on, we can learn something about Lartigue and his age, about photography and the imagination, and.
—My notebook's in my rucksack, Walt said. Where's a pen? *If the god Eros.* Hey! Here are the lost underpants, in the rucksack.
—Ah yes, Marc said. I remember.
—*Wild thyme and meadow dill between his toes.*
—I put that in for you, O Sniffer. The fig simile was for Cyril.
—Down near Les Éyzies, in the Gorge d'Enfer, there's an outdoor zoo of prehistoric animals, or their great-grandchildren, and there's a long-haired goat, with oblong yellow eyes and a beard like God's. Maman said he may *be* God. And balls like two

Perrier bottles in a shopping bag. And absolutely the strongest and outrageousest stink in the whole world. We had to hold onto each other just to stand up. Sam was real brave to breathe at all. The King of Fuckers, Daisy said. So that's goat. You've mixed it with olive. You once said seaweed and olive.
—I give up, Marc said.
—Mna, Walt said. Speak up, Cyril. We're democrats.
—Both?
—Arcadia, Marc said. I can read minds. Me, I need a shower and to brush my teeth and move my bowels and shave.
—Don't shave, Walt said.

20

Marc's apartment was different in lamplight, the kitchen more polychrome modern brilliantly lit, the study cozier. They'd had a walk along the river after supper, when Walt snuck his hand into Marc's. He and Sam held hands.
—We got you, he had said, because of us. After your first night Maman asked me if I understood and I gave her a very positive set of nods.
—I was convinced I'd got to heaven before my time.
—In bed for three days, as I remember.
—Learning to be a satyr, half out of my mind. I had known that you were there, a damned nuisance. Here I was with the first woman who knew as much as God about sex, maybe more, and was lovely and intelligent and kind, but with a brat somewhere around the apartment. It was late on the second afternoon, when I'd fucked more than ever in my life before, and was having trouble believing it all, when Penny put me in one of her bathrobes, first clothes I'd had on in fifty-six hours, to meet not one but two brats in identical yellow sweat shirts and wickedly short denim pants, identical haircuts, and barefoot. Penny seemed to be amused to introduce us.
—We knew you didn't know, and resented you as much as you

wished we didn't exist, but the game made it fun. And Maman played it cool. Marc she said you had for a name, and introduced us as Sam and Walt, best friends, and showed you how we all have a family conference at four, with milk and cookies for us and tea for Maman. You hadn't shaved, and really didn't know how to talk to us. But of course if Maman liked you, we had to, too, and afterwards we decided that because you were young and goodlooking and, as Bee said, cute, we had no objections. You were scared, and we were hoping that it was us who scared you.

They admired an Alsatian watchdog on a barge, nudged each other when American tourists passed in awful clothes. Marc asked if they were to return to his place and got a big-eyed silly smile from Walt.

—We have to, don't we?

—Whatever that means. I think I see.

21

The rain had set in as steady and continuous as time itself well before Marc walked Walt home at seven in the morning.

—The god Eros is wet to the knackers, Marc said to Penny, who was in slacks and sweater and sipping coffee, as he kept skipping and darting from under the umbrella. I'm only soaked from the knees south.

—Off everything, this minute, she said to Walt with a kiss, and to Marc with a hug and kiss, shoes and jeans. I've had the most marvellous night's sleep, down at the bottom of the unconcious, and am, I hope, the more rested of us three. There are croissants, the fig jam Daisy paid so much for, and country butter.

She put a finger to a cheek to admire and smile at Marc in sweater and briefs.

—Lines for Masaccio, a Tuscan youth in jerkin and codpiece.

Walt, towelling his hair and sneezing, appeared in a plaid dressing gown.

—Memo, Penny said in her business voice, a change of Marc's clothes for here, and jammies and togs, and a toothbrush, for Walt at Marc's.

Marc stared before he grinned.

—And don't emit aspersions about women. I know my son. He's radiantly happy.

—What about me?

—You look a bit as Walt would look if he were not the exemplar in our time of innocence and candor.

—I *am?* Walt said, buttering a farl of croissant and filling his mouth.

—If we talk while chewing we sound like a German tourist.

—God knows what he is, Penny. Some elemental force that Greeks and Romans tamed before they dared to start in on the groundwork of civilization.

—Has he bewitched you? It's the eyes. *I'm* going to the Delaunay.

—With me and Sam, I hope, and Marc. Is Daisy coming too?

—The whole gang is welcome, but going I am, and elemental forces can behave themselves.

Walt, guddling inside his bathrobe, wiping fig jam from his lips, went to the phone in the hall, where they heard the bird cheep of kissing sounds, a conspirator's chuckle, various phrases in argot which they took on faith to be salacious, and *sure, right now.* He returned with volume two of the Praeger Encyclopedia of Art, saying Delaunay, Delaunay.

—*The Cardiff Team,* Penny was saying, and Rousseau's football players, what do you think? Sonia's circles, the whole Russian dimension.

22

Jean-Luc, massaging sleep from his eyelids and yawning like a lion, had got as far as changing into a fresh sweatshirt, and stood spraddle-legged in socks, belt undone and dangling, fly spread open 180 degrees.

—*Jour,* he said. Both the boys. The general will be bewitched. He prolongs his swim and callisthenics when Monsieur Walt isn't here, hoping that he will come. And now Monsieur Sam.

They had met at a brasserie two days before, Walt recognizing Jean-Luc in jeans, sweater, and Danish student cap before Jean-Luc placed Walt. An exchange of hand signals meaning *but of course,* the introduction of Sam as best friend, a pleasantry about not spotting people you know naked when they have clothes on, with exchanges of who lives where, and agreement that Monsieur was a thoroughly sympathetic sort. Did Monsieur Sam know him? Oh yes. They were all of a friendship around Walt's mother. Sam was, Jean-Luc handsomely said, welcome at the Hermès when there was no one but Messieurs Marc and Walt, and the very old general who was keeping fit for when the unspeakable German swine invaded France next, an outrage to be expected at any moment. One was required to be fifteen for membership, and as Monsieur Walt was advanced for his age, which he wasn't asking, the same point could be stretched for Walt's best friend.

—Sam talked about meeting you the better part of dinner, Marc said. They can use the same towel.

—We're not stingy here, Jean-Luc said, tossing three towels Marc's way, caught by Sam, whose frank eyes studied his naked legs and sex.

Walt's eyes said *be brave.* Marc screened Sam's undressing, so that when Jean-Luc was greeting and unbuttoning the general, they were all in the pool, Marc crawling with long strokes beside two elvishly supple breast-strokers and frog-kickers, squealing.

The general was delighted. Yet another healthy young male over whose shoulder the lanyard would proudly loop.

—The other's friend, you say? Charming they are together, will you not agree, Jean-Luc? From good families, too. You can tell. You can always tell.

THE FIELD PATH

The badger's path from sett to sett, the auroch's to the pond, sheepwalks older than history, hunters' trails. Rome's empire was a system of roads. A walk in the country is a game. Walt and Sam can quickly turn it into one, playing at tag, racing each other, finding, exploring. Walt wants hawthorn to have a smell, but says that the bitter green odor of goldweed makes up for it.

24

Marc in black jeans with white stitching outlining the pockets and fly, gray sweatshirt, ribbed white socks and running shoes had turned up mid-afternoon.
—Briefcase, Walt said, so you've come back to work. Mama's at Daisy's and will be along in awhile. Sam and I just got in from mucking about. Want some American peanut butter and jam on sliced bread?
—Hello, Sam, Marc said, or is it Bee? A T-shirt from The University of Harvard, which seems to be your sole garment, waffles on gender.
—Sam, Walt said.
—Bee, Sam said, showing that the T-shirt was indeed her only garment.
—Marc's blushing, Walt said. Here, have a bite of my sandwich. It gums up your mouth so that you can't talk. I'll bet you'd like some wine and cheese.
—Don't think, O Mice, that I didn't see the millisecond eyelock between you two.
—Well, Walt said, kneeling to untie Marc's shoelace, we know how it is with you. You've shaved since the seminar this morning, and changed into germ-free clothes, and your ears are still pink from a shower, and your toes will smell of talcum.
Sam was unlacing the other shoe, and each pulled off a sock.

—Flowery talcum, Walt said. Lavender and almonds.
—If Jean-Luc at the gym, with the big hang-down, Sam said, has two girls, I wonder if he loves both of them every day, or one on Monday, the other on Tuesday, and so on. You unbuckle and unbutton, Walt. I'll do the zipper.
Each was hauling on a jeans leg when Penny arrived.
—We're saving you time, Walt said.
—I'm not looking, Penny said on her way to the kitchen. I think I saw two half-naked children playing ragdoll with my assistant Monsieur Marc Bordeaux, also half-naked.
—Jean-Luc looks bright, and is probably very talented. I'll bet he thinks about one girl for awhile, when he's helping the general peel off his long johns, her cute navel, and then switches over to the other, her wiggly tongue or whichwhat.
—We're playing Jean-Luc and The Old General at the gym. He's about a hundred, and swims like a dog. Later, when more people are there to swim and work out, Marc says that Jean-Luc wears a *microslip*, but for the general he's Greek Olympics.
—The general says that *slips de bain* are scandalous.
—And, Penny said from the kitchen, when Jean-Luc's Lucille and his Anne-Marie find out about each other, we will have the great French plot for a novel. I see that you've bereft the general of his last stitch. May I borrow him after a while?

25

Knowing how to live involves finding out. When Daisy's friend the widow Courcy offered her little house in the country as a place for weekends, Daisy, Penny, Walt, and Sam took the train out to it, fell in love with it, and began to make it their retreat. There was a large kitchen looking out on an orchard with high hedges all around, two small downstairs rooms out of Mother Goose, and up a steep and narrow stair two bedrooms with fireplaces. Jules and Louise Maigret's cottage at Meung-sur-

Loire Penny called it. Fourier and Kropotkin would rub their hands with approval. Mice squeaked in the smaller bedroom where Sam and Walt spent their first night there. Spent, not slept, Sam said, as the feather tick and the wood fire and the smell of the country through the windows and an owl and the strangeness of being in a new place kept them awake and talking most of the night.
—For two whole days, Penny said to Walt on the country road from the train, no streets, no subways, no telephone.
—Just us.
—Tons of quiet. You're not going to be bored?
—Not me. You said once, maybe I wasn't supposed to be listening, that teenagers are not friends with their parents and tear off on their own, and that you can only be friends with your children before they sprout pubic hair. Well, I'm going to be friends with you all our lives, you'll see.

ORCHARD

Marc in deck chair, soaking up photons, Walt in random motion.
—These trees are as old as time. Apple and pear. Planted by the Romans. Some of the patch we're to weed out used to be, I think, parsley and basil, gone wild. I like the moss on the bricks. Smell my fingers.
—Licorice, Marc said without opening his eyes.
—It's taking over, back yonder. The seeds have velcro hooks.
—Glycyrrhiza glabra, *la réglisse*. Sweetroot. One of the most individual of aromas.
—Even if I got to be friends with him, Walt said from somewhere way behind, Christofer probably wouldn't let me sniff. His aftershave, Sam says, is tacky, elk sperm he thinks it is. But there are horsy smells to his sweaters and shirts.
—How voices carry in this quiet, which has a kind of resonance of its own. Listen.
—I've never sniffed a Norwegian.

—Penny says that we'll hear no more of your nose's curiosity when you find out that there are people who are far less scrupulous about bathing than us.
—That's what would be interesting. What if Christofer's socks are really gross, like the lion cages at the Vincennes zoo? Do we need anything from Felix Potin? Is there a book for giving a name to all these midges and flies and gnats?
—Walt.
—*Adsum.* Here in what I think is mint. Square stem, yes?
—Square stem is mint. Walt, I'm wholly honest and friendly in wanting to understand you.
—Now I'm a problem.
—By understand I think I mean learn. Kropotkin and Fourier are all very well, and the horse and common sense that Penny invokes with such authority, though it's my private opinion that the four of you made it all up, but I, with poor Christofer, come from outside, like lambs to the shearing, innocent and muddled.
—Baa.

Marc sat up, taking off his sunglasses, rubbing an ankle and thinking. Walt, an eyebrow cocked, ran his tongue along his upper lip.
—Come over, Marc said, so's I can smell your licorice fingers again.
—Well, there's mint too, now, and if that's basil, basil, and on my peter as well.
—How did that happen?
—Couldn't say. My toes should be the most interesting, all the herbs and leaf trash and grass. In the Dutch magazine from the kiosk on the Wagram big brother with the denim-blue eyes and jeans rusting out in the crotch masturbates little brother often and continually, according to the dictionary and my decoding of the grammar, and in betweentimes, I think it says, when big brother is with his very friendly friends, little brother masturbates himself constantly and happily, two more Dutch adverbs. They both have wonderfully big feet, these loving brothers, and economy-size dicks.

—And it's your warmhearted belief that little brother will go crazy with happiness before he has hair in his britches.
—He has some already. Big brother has a neat tight clump, like you and Jean-Luc at the gym.
Marc sighed a smile, pulled Walt close, and kissed his navel.
—You really did flavor your peter with licorice. Your knees are trembling, scout.
—Going crazy.
—You smell like sunshine, grass, and boy.

27

The Rolls having slid away, Cyril scampered up to Marc's making a clatter on the stairs that pleased the concierge. Monsieur *le petit* used to be of a solemnity, grave.
He was taking off his tie as Marc let him in.
—Heard your typewriter on the way up, he said, after his cheerful *hullo*.
—I don't see how, Marc said. Bragging in a letter to an old friend about the way I live now, leaving out a good half. He wouldn't believe it.
Cyril was in the bedroom putting his shirt, jacket, and trousers on hangers. From the box in the corner on which Sam had printed CYRIL'S BATMAN TOGS he took a red polo shirt, a pair of short white pants, blue tall socks, briefs *style micro,* and scruffy sneakers, once Walt's.
—Forty push-ups this morning, he said.

28

Penny, tucked up in her chair, was reading Simenon's *Le Charretier de la "Providence"*. The country day, radiant, blue-skied, and warm, was moving toward noon. She and Walt had set out at dawn, taking a train from the Étoile to Vernon, where they'd had coffee in the square, and walked the eight kilometres to the cottage, speaking to cows, horses, and postmen on bicycles. Walt was a lively conversationalist all the way out. *In the stable the only horse left was the one the proprietor harnessed to go to market, a big gray animal as friendly as a dog, which was not tied up and occasionally ambled about the yard, among the hens.*

Walt, barefoot, was raking an old flower bed from which he pulled weeds and grass.

—I get the dirt all turned over and mixed up good, right?

A hundred metres away, a little Decauville train travelled back and forth across a lumberyard, and its driver, at the rear of the little engine, had set up a large umbrella under which he stood with his shoulders hunched.

—Yes. You want it soft and deep. Your back looks like a Swedish ginger cookie.

—All the rest of me will, too, soon as I get the seeds in. Zinnias and asters. Dirt between the toes feels great.

—It's probably too late in the year to be planting zinnias and asters, but we won't be discouraged. Make a divot with the trowel, dollop in water, and put a few seeds in.

—And hope and watch.

Two horses were being led by a little girl between eight and ten, wearing a red dress and carrying her doll at arm's length.

—Trowel, trowel. That's in the shed. Where are the seed packets?

—Behind you, in the sack. If you throw away all your clothes, as you seem to be doing, you'll play with yourself and forget horticulture.

—Mna. Well, maybe some, for the fun of it . I've got to be an Iroquois planting maize in Ohio. A bucket of water from the kitchen.

—And a cup for ladling in, slowly. Then make a little hillock over each one.

—When will my wizzle be dark-skinned, winey blue, with big veins, like Marc's?

—When you're Marc's age, I imagine. Nature looks after such things.

—With Marc's help.

—Fill the bucket about half, or it will be too heavy. Marc is envious of you. He says he was backward, shy, and inhibited. I can't get a clear picture of his parents. Nice, ordinary people, as best I can make out.
—And then we got him. He's still shy. It's sort of nice.
—I know. I don't think he quite believes us. Do you think, since you're being so practical, that you might bring out the thermos of soup, two bowls, the packets of sandwiches, spoons, for a *fête champêtre* here in the orchard?
—By Poulenc.

29

Walt had brought out two blankets, for sunbathing.
—That tractor you can just hear, he said, is as close as anybody is, so we can lie in the sun like Danes in their backyards, New Caledonians. You can't see through the hedge without sticking your head through, which a boy all freckles did once when Marc and I were out here.
—Seeing a beautiful little boy and a beautiful big boy either soaking up sunshine or doing things he's still thinking about.
—I'm not a little boy, am I, and Marc's grown all the way up, isn't he?
—He's a big boy.
—I may have been petting my mouse, to make him feel loved. Marc likes being my big brother, you know?
—Daisy thinks it's wonderful, what I've told her of it. Walt, sweetheart, as long as we're having an orgy of country life, frolicking in Arcadia, what I'd like is another coffee and the merest sip of the armagnac that's in the cupboard. And a pillow. One at a time, and you won't have to leave off throttling your mouse. Where do I spread the blankets? Here?
—Be right back, mouse and I, coffee first. One sugar, right?
Walt returned, walking on eggs, coffee in one hand, brandy in the other, pillow balanced on his head.
—Sam will be jealous when I tell him I got to bring you three

things at once. The waiter at the Balzac could bring six more coffees and a platter of ham and cheese.
—All this sweet quiet is doing things to me, Penny said. The age of this orchard is not like the age of buildings and streets in cities. The old pear tree, there, knows that it exists, whereas the Tour Eiffel doesn't. It must have some exhilaration in its blossoms and leaves and pears. It likes rain and sunshine, and draws into itself away from frost and sharp winds. The Romans brought them here, along with apples, and the Romans got them from the Greeks. They come from the very old civilizations in Persia, and maybe from as far away as China.
—I'll put that in the notebook later.
—You brought it?
—Goes with me everywhere, Sam writes in it, too. Sam *hears* things that I let get by. And then there are things you don't see the importance of until days later. I can be real dumb. Aren't you going to take everything off?
—If you think the locals won't fall through the hedge and hurt themselves. I'm having what I call my long memories, a Proustian kind of return to an experience that Spinoza called a third kind of knowing. Marc was fascinated when I explained it to him.
—Spinoza, Walt said. Somebody way back.
—A philosopher, Dutch, from a Jewish family, seventeenth century. Marc can tell you more than you want to know about him. He wrote a lot about how we know and feel the world and ourselves. He hated messy thinking and messy feelings. But he allowed for imagination and intuition as a way of knowing. We have experiences about experiences long past, memories that return all by themslves. When you were fetching my pillow and brandy and coffee, I suddenly remembered nursing you, and the sensual delight of your earnest, oh so greedy sucking, watching me out of the side of your eyes. It was then that I came all over silly and began to relive being a girl of ten with my doll. It was wonderfully sexual, this feeling, and I was all at once ten and a

mother with a real warm smiling feeding baby. Am I making any sense? It's poetical, spontaneous, not to be talked about with any clarity. All the lovemaking that went into your conception melted into the hideous pain of your birth, and it all became the one complex pleasure, of which you were the existential reassurance. The wholeness of experience is a secret until such moments. Of course it may all have been your happiness at the teat spilling over into me. I remember thinking: I must keep this moment. I'll need it later on.

—I was your doll, Walt said. I looked at you out of the side of my eyes, like this?

—Yes, but you were much wiser. Babies are. They know everything.

—And then I forgot it all. Are there more of these Spinoza's minutes? Maybe I'll have one.

—Oh yes. When you first dressed Bee in your clothes and invented Sam, it made me remember when I envied boys their clothes. These intuitive waking dreams have something to do with the sources of art, as mine have the visionary intensity of Redon or Palmer or Burchfield. Marc says they're mystical. I don't think so. The mystical is mush. My intuitive moments are a reward for having paid attention in the first place.

—Bee invented Sam. Maybe I did. We invented Sam together.

—Your mouse looks happy, and is considerably bigger than any mouse I've ever seen. A young cucumber, more like.

—A parsnip beside Marc's. Cyril's is an asparagus stalk.

—Daisy likes to remember when you and Bee first saw each other naked, on the beach in Denmark, brown as ginger cookies, with wondering eyes but sneakily cool, wrecked between polite indifference and raging curiosity.

—This orchard is magic, you know? I've lived under that bush over there for a thousand years.

—The hydrangea.

—Yes, and I come here from Paris at night, in about five seconds. That moss on the roof, with the mustard in with the green,

I like to hover just above it. I sink through the roof and the bedrooms to the kitchen, which is cold and dark except for moonlight on the hearth and table. But the best part is flying back, over the train tracks, and being snug and warm in bed. Night air is chilly and damp.

30

Walt, having cubed a bite of melon, fed it to Bee, while chewing a bite of melon she'd just fed him.

—Cyril would like to see this, Marc said. Our outing in Saint-Germain was a sort of dream for him, poor little fellow.

—He's one strange kid, I'm here to tell you.

—Let me get some of it straight, Penny said. You dressed him in Walt's clothes that he keeps at Marc's.

—All except underpants, the which he was wearing a pair of that come way up to here, and practically had legs to them.

—And you went by train, conspuing the chauffeur, and did the museum.

—Where, Marc said, Walt and Sam kept their hands on each other's butts most of the time, showing off for Cyril, and eliciting great interest from a young German who hadn't bathed in some weeks.

—And had lunch in the English garden place, and walked in the forest.

—Where, Walt said, Jean-Jacques Rousseau used to muck about, giving Marc his cue to lecture us on him, and we had to distract Cyril while Sam had a pee.

—And had a wonderful time, Marc and his three young friends, and got home in good time to change Cyril back into his wholly inappropriate suit and deliver him to this chauffeur keeper. And here you are. I got some very forward work done on *L'Equipe Cardiff,* and Daisy and I had tea, before big Christofer turned up, looking more Norwegian than ever. He'd been playing football with some Dutch and Danes and smelled like a horse.

So I suggested that Bee do bed and breakfast here. Did I do right?

—Absolutely, Bee said.

—Me, too? Marc asked.

—O wow! Walt said. I love days like this. A great explore, and then all the beds full overnight. Cyril's probably in his nightgown, and the chauffeur is taking his temperature to see if he's running a fever from walking miles in a forest and a drafty museum with big handsome Marc and two nifty nasty boys.

—I wonder, Penny said, putting out cognac. His mother has simply left, perfectly understandable if you've met Ducasse, who seems to have been born and raised in a bank. But however desperately unhappy I was, I couldn't leave Walt. There must be some species of housekeeper, or maybe there's a new mother in the wings.

—All Cyril needs, Marc said, is a stepmother. I got him to hold hands when crossing the street, and he put his arm over my shoulder when Sam and Walt were seducing each other in public to cheek some rather sullen and unhappy Americans. But he loosened up as the afternoon went on. Walt climbed me, of course, and rode for a while on my shoulders, and then Sam, but not Cyril.

Walt sniffed Penny's brandy. Bee, Marc's.

—We're in for mischief, Penny said. I know the signs.

—Stay where you are, Bee said. We'll be back.

A whispered consultation.

—No need to go offstage, Walt said. We've got it. Madame et Monsieur, a mime by Walt and Sam.

Sam stood at attention. Walt, as if seeing her for the first time, swinging one leg up and around, and the other, turning as he walked, circled Sam and stopped, taking a stance beside her, and like her, at attention. He looked at her sideways, clicking his eyes back to a forward stare when she caught him trying to look at her. She with the same furtive slide of eyes, after an interval, tried to look at him undetected.

—Something Beckettian, Penny said.
Sam took a step forward and recited:

> The gorgeous peacock struts and flirts
> And drags his tail, but when his mind
> On peahens dwells he lifts his skirts
> And shows all Persia his behind.

—Apollinaire! Marc said.
Sam stepped back, Walt forward.

> My poor owl of a heart has failed,
> Its fervent heat is at an end.
> I've been nailed, unnailed, and renailed.
> But all who love me, I commend.

Applause from Penny and Marc.

Walt and Sam faced each other, nose to nose. They about-faced, standing butt to butt, listening. The gritty slide of Sam's zipper brought Walt's fingers to his.

—Danish television, Marc said.

Walt turned to face Sam's back, pushing up her polo shirt. She raised her arms for him to pull it over her head. They turned, Sam hauling off Walt's shirt. They turned again, Sam holding her arms up to have Walt's shirt put on her. Walt, Sam's. Meanwhile, both had been losing their kneepants to gravity, until they were around their ankles. Each kicked them aside. They pulled down, and off, each other's underwear.

—Now Sam's Bee, Penny said, though who knows with these two.

Walt spoke:

> All admire my distinguished grace,
> My lines so noble that the Greeks
> Thought light had voice in my face,
> About which Trismegistus speaks.

—That's Orpheus, Marc said. There's no Eurydice in the suite, is there? Prepare to blush, Penny.

Bee, one hand on her sex, the other on Walt's:

I, a bunny, know another
I would like to kiss all over.
He's as loving as a brother
In his warren in the clover.

Both bowed. End of mime. Applause.

HENRY DE MONTHERLANT

Such heavy leather shoes for legs
so young and slender to end in,
the only bulk to a body
so lightly clad. To pull them from
his messy gym bag where they've lain
under muddy and grass-stained shorts,
is to hear the coach's whistle
slice the air, the field crack, to take
from the private musk of a sack
the cold light of a winter day
and hold victory in my hands.
So inert, so slight to the eye,
these flying kicking, living shoes
obeyed the fierce will of a boy
who could fight back a hero's tears.
Still oiled, still spattered with dried mud,
they've kept their strong seaweed odor.
In their scuffed heft, copper grommets,
and essence of brute elegance,
they are as noble as the field
they trod and the boy who wore them.
The ankles are bulged like the boss

of a Greek shield, the instep his.
Could I not know whose shoes these were?
To cup the hard heels in my hands
is to feel them full of bright fire.

THE FIELD PATH: OLD PEAR TREE BY ATGET

This grass, with knotted roots and plaited halms, has outlasted centuries of wars, boots and shells, tank treads and bombs. *Herba est, gramen et pabulum.* Birds, Roman boots, the wind seeded it here. It is the ancestor of bread. Walt, wrinkling his nose, says that we need a sheep to crop it, as in the Bois. I ask him to talk about grass, he says he must be naked to do it, like Adam, and hops to wiggle his briefs off his lifted ankle. Grass is, he says, well, grass. well attested and beyond quibble. It grows on the ground, most anywhere. Cows and horses eat it. It is green. His namesake Whitman in America wrote a book about it. It makes meadows, with flowers mixed in, and ants, grasshoppers, and butterflies. It feels good to walk on it barefoot, in summer. It is and isn't a weed.

33

Marc, awake, spread his fingers through Walt's hair.
—I've been awake, edging out of a crazy dream about a place I've never seen, a road, with lots of bridges, through a forest in Sweden, with old-fashioned globe streetlamps on the bridges. If I wake before you, I can study one thing and another.
—I'll bet.
—Well, I can. Like how much your face grew whiskers in the night.
—Let's have a pee, huh? And find coffee. The day's all ours.
—Cyril said he thought he could get away from his keepers before they let him loose for the Lartigue show.
—The day's still all ours.

—You think?
—Hold up your arms, Marc said, and I'll slide a sweater on you.
—Gulp of golden pulpy orange juice first. Poor Cyril. No friends to dress him.
—Not everybody's as lucky as us. I need socks. It's chilly. And briefs.
—Coffee's ready. Have you looked outside? It's pissing rain. Socks sound good. Veto briefs.
—Can't find yours, anyhow. I forget if you dispensed with them in the study, the bedroom, or on the stairs coming in.

Walt, mouth full of Danish, pouring coffee, scrunched his eyebrows in a frown.

Doorbell.

—Cyril this early?
—His mind's gone. Hopeless case.
—Yes? Marc said into the intercom. *Bonjour*. But of course! Come on up.
—Bathrobe? Walt said. Poor Cyril.
—Civilized deference.

34

Somebody was playing *The Sunflower Slow Drag* on the piano.
—My God! Penny said, jolted awake, the little shits are playing Scott Joplin at six in the morning.
—More like seven, Marc said. Is it a revolt?

Through the bedroom door, Bee backwards, bringing a tray of coffee, croissants, butter, and gooseberry jam.

—Good morining, everybody, she said. Walt's bringing orange juice. He wanted me to come in to music.

CHLAMYS

Perpendicular summer sun made the old orchard a Pissarro. Marc had brought out a notebook, the *Anthology,* and a Greek dictionary. Walt followed with a long lap rug for lying on.

—It's one of the poems dedicating things to a god. A gardener retiring would place his rake, hoe, and clippers before a statue of Priapos. This one, by Theodoros, is one where a young man is offering his boyhood gear to Hermes Korophilos, that is, lover of boys. What, Walt, are you doing?
—Keeping the tone in my peter with some good slow pulls. Greek boy, what age, is taking his top and marbles to church. This is for Penny, right?
—She wants intersections of sports and Eros. Turn around and look at the text. What age? Well, boyhood's over: he has a crop of pubic hair, or *ephebaion*, and is thus an *ephebos*, no longer a *pais*. So in the first line we have finely carded lamb's wool, the material of his felt broad-brimmed hat.
—One boy's hat.
—Then his doubled-back clasp, a sort of big safety pin for holding his chlamys on at the shoulder. It was a short shirt, just covering one's butt, and was rather liberally unfastened in front.
—They were nice people, the old Greeks.
—Then his strigil, here called a *stlenggis*.
—For squidging off oil and dust after wrestling.
—He's keeping his oil flask. It would have been shaped like a cock and scrotum, realistically modelled, with a small handle in back for a thong, and presumably a cork stopper. Olive oil flavored with dill or lavender.
—Better and better.
—Then his bow, and never-not-thrown ball, and his slingshot, and his worn-to-a-frazzle chlamys, which is *gloiopotin*, which I've seen translated *sweat-soaked*.
—Yummy.
—But *gloios* is the gunk the strigil scrapes off: oil and sweat and wrestling-floor dust. *For a well-spent boyhood.*
—And this was show-and-tell for the god Hermes? For whom your gym is named.
—Misnamed, isn't it?

INFINITE BUT LIMITED

Streaks of mud and halms of grass on their jerseys Marc's left knee barked, Walt's right cheek scuffed and socks falling down, they took off their shoes caked with clay outside the concierge's lodge, enjoying her smiling approval. Monsieur Bordeaux's manners were exemplary, as witness the paper of flowers he brought her from time to time, his willingness to exchange interesting news from the neighborhood, and his promptness in paying his rent.

—Always stay on the good side of concierges, Marc said in his apartment.

—I keep telling Sam, Walt said, pushing Marc into the bedroom, that, yes, *Robinson Crusoe* is almost as good as a book can get, but *Don Quijote* is better. We once, way back, thought *The Mysterious Island* was the best book in the world. Sam says *Don Quijote* doesn't go in a straight line and that *Robinson Crusoe* does. Don't dare move: stand right there.

—Before you get into things allowed only by friends and very friendly brothers, enrich a washrag with hot soapy water, fetch the bottle of rubbing alcohol, iodine, the roll of gauze, and the roll of tape. And get some antiseptic salve for your cheek.

—Sam should be here. He loves playing doctor. Soap and water. You did a number on your knee, for sure. Scraped it raw.

—Oof! Pat the alcohol on with your fingers. Let me do it.

—No. I'm doing it. This iodine's going to sting something awful. Need scissors for the gauze. Scissors, scissors. Sam may be right about *Robinson Crusoe,* you know? You can imagine being Robinson, especially on a rainy day or out in the country, but not Don Quijote. Hold the tape while I cut it. What the concierge likes is the way your shorts prod out in front.

—Imagining yourself as Robinson Crusoe is acting like Don Quijote, isn't it? Go wash your face and smear salve on it.

—OK, but don't move. Stay right where you are, like Calixte Delmas on his monument. I did a number on my face, too.

—We could both improve the ecology of the apartment by having a shower.
—When I get you undressed. Lean over and off comes your jersey. Suck in, and down come your shorts. Hold up leg: one long sock, whiffy in the toe. Other leg. Flip jockstrap inside out and slide down.
—Poke snoot into cup of jockstrap, snuffling.
—Don't make fun of the retarded.
—Retarded! Walt, you're some kind of genius. Just what kind, God knows. Do I get to undress you?
—Do you have to, you mean.
—Friends are friends.
—There was an afternoon, once, when Sam and I dressed and undressed each other for like an hour. Penny said that there were brighter people in the insane asylum. You're distending and enlarging.
—When Cocteau was younger than you he saw a boy naked for the first time, in the country, at a farm, and fainted dead away.
—A really good-looking kid, was he? No brothers, no locker rooms, no swimming pools?
—Not back then. I imagine a gawky thatch-topped boy with red elbows and knees, dog-paddling in the duck pond. It's a case of classical panic, of meeting up with Pan, when your heart jumps up into your throat.
—When I first saw you, friend Marc, I felt real funny and strange, jealous and resentful too. Sam said you were handsome, and Sam and I sort of share a mind, as you know. Your hair was a wreck, your eyes were all eyelashes, and you had a silly grin. You had on Penny's dressing gown.
—You are like your mother, a very loving person. Hold your arms up, for the removal of a grimy and grassy jersey.
—Fainted dead away. Probably scared the shit out of the farm boy. Leave socks till last.
—Talk about things poking out.
—We're going to be in the shower together, right?

—That's your Coquelin *cadet* smile, as Penny calls it. Eyes squinched, chin out, mouth a wiggle. It would be a smirk on a less handsome face. Sam can do an exavr imitation of it. Mussed hair plays its part. In Vuillard's lithograph Coquelin's wearing an auburn wig of cascading curls.

—Would I make Cocteau faint?

—Dead away.

—So would you. Fix the water, half hot, half cold. The soap smells like an oil rag, furniture polish, Lysol, paraffin. Will your tape come off?

—It says it's waterproof. Tape over hair doesn't ever come off. That would be too easy. Sam's going to be jealous of your skinned cheek.

—That would be Cyril. Sam will become Bee, and look at the ceiling, like Penny.

37

Marc, awake after a dream by Delvaux of familiar stone streets and Balkan houses where he'd never been, of people naked and clothed whom he recognized in shifting identities, an agreeable dream of beautiful fugitive images, sat up in bed, stretched, and yawned. One might as well try to put fog in a sack as retain the euphoria of a dream, but wisps of it stuck to his soul as he peed and washed his face and put on water for coffee. He wore only his shirt of the day before, unbuttoned.

And who would be ringing his doorbell so early?

Cyril.

—I said we were setting out at eight to learn the names of trees in the Bois de Vincennes.

—I see, Marc said. The names of trees. Come in, squirt. Have you had any breakfast?

—I said we were all going to have breakfast at a *bistrot*.

—Coffee's dripping through. Rolls and jam, OK? I'll skip my swim. Or I could take you along.

—I can't swim. Nobody's taught me. Can I have breakfast, like you, in just a shirt? I need to change into Walt's clothes, anyhow, and can stop halfway.

Marc, in the afterglow of his dream and idly toying with his naked glans, put another cup on the table, and found rolls and jam in the cabinet.

—I think I see how it is with you, friend Cyril. I'm in a shirt because I've just got up and like to hang free, for the fun of it.

—Me, too, Cyril said, though I've never got to do it.

—Do it.

—I've never really liked anybody the way I like Sam and Walt, and you.

—And yourself. You must like yourself.

—I like myself.

—Cyril, you're an intelligent boy, with brains. Lacan, the psychiatrist, says that people your age and younger have a private sexuality and that with it you have a deep-lying dread that it will go away, that you will use it up. It will actually, as you grow up, become something else, much better and sexier. I'm, as you know, Penny's lover, and I'll bet you can't even begin to think of Penny as being sexy.

—I can, sort of. You're sexy, and if Penny likes you, then she's sexy.

—We wouldn't be talking at all if there weren't a lacunarity to my own growing up, not that I've got there yet.

—Lacunarity.

—Experiences that got left out. But then we all have our own way of growing up, of finding ourselves.

—Yes.

—Butter first, like this, then jam, for a big bite. Don't you have rolls for breakfast at home?

—We have cream of wheat, with cream and slices of banana, or soft-boiled eggs in a cup, with Melba toast. I like jam and rolls lots better. Tickles the back of your throat. What do Sam and Walt get for breakfast?

—If they're at Penny's, croissants and hot chocolate, with orange juice, deconstructing *Le Figaro,* talking to each other in gibberish. Penny has one of her notebooks on the table, as ideas have done things in her head overnight. I'm not really sure what they do when I'm not there. They're very witty together, those three. I don't know what goes on at Daisy's. I hear obscure jokes about Christofer. And Daisy gets at her painting early.

—They don't fuss at each other?

—I don't think so. Quarrel, you mean?

—Get mad and call each other names.

—I can't imagine it. They're all too good-natured and honest. There are frictions of course, nobody's an angel, but when there's trouble, a wreck Penny calls it, they have a kind of traffic court. The vectors of the collision are charted, the damage is assessed. Apologies and hugs ensue. Walt usually accuses himself of having acted like a German, or an American. Justice, friendliness, and *bon ton* are restored. Penny comes down hard on selfishness. Or the infringement of somebody else's rights.

—You mean they can *say* what they think isn't right?

—I think so, yes. When I first met Penny I was brought home as a resident stud, a lover, and allowances were made for me, as if I were an untrained puppy. And then a very subtle education got under way. I was in shock, I think. I still am, a little bit.

—Yes.

—What do you mean, *yes?*

—I mean I'm listening. Sam says the worst thing you can do is not to listen.

VICENTE HUIDOBRO: FOR ROBERT DELAUNAY (1918)

O Tour Eiffel the sky's guitar
thy tiptop wireless telegraph
gathers words as a rosebush bees

it does not flow at night the Seine
a bugle or a telescope
Tour Eiffel a beehive of words

or an inkpot full of honey
at dawn a spider with steel thread
weaves its web in the morning fog

my little boy climbs the tower
as a singer mounts through the scale
do re mi fa sol la ti do

thus we are high up in the air
a bird sings in the antenna
into Europe's electric wind

that blows hats off way below us
they can fly but they cannot sing
Jacqueline O daughter of France

what do you see from there so high
the Seine sleeps under its bridges
I see the earth turn and I blow

my trumpet toward all the seas
and to your perfume bees and words
come over the four horizons

farther than your song can be heard
I am the dawn queen of the poles
I am the rose of the four winds

that engolden autumn and bring
snow and that rose's death is mine
year long a bird sings in my head

all this is what the Tower said
this aviary of the world
a campanile for Paris

her trademark poised in the wide sky
and on the day of Victory
she will stand there among the stars

39

Walt, having pulled his mouth into an ogre's grin for the street below, with trollish dance, kissed his mother good morning while placing *Le Figaro* by her plate, saying that what he liked about Marc's trousers is that whereas they fit perfectly, snug in the waist and butt, they were taxed for room in front.

—Well yes, Penny said sipping coffee. As a woman and a fool I think a virile member tending to the horizontal complements pleasantly his intelligent eyes and cute nose. But it's you I adore, sweetheart. Marc is for fun.

Walt thought about this with cocked head.

—He's neat. Can he be my friend as much as yours?

—Whyever not? The one thing that's truly infinite is the imagination, and that's the big component in desire, isn't it? Friendship, or love, has its good will built into it, that's its nature. Marc and I have a hundred ways of being friendly, going to bed with him being one of them.

—And arguing about space in Piero della Francesca.

—Good pronunciation. We aren't arguing, sweet. We are discussing.

—O and K. Gotcha. There's the door. It's Bee, I think.

Bee it was, in newspaperboy's cap, jacket, British scarf, and kneepants.

—I can match everything, Walt said, kissing her on the nose, except the ragamuffin headgear.

—I saw Marc, I'm pretty certain, dancing through traffic at the roundabout, so I didn't wave.

—Then we're having a party for breakfast, Penny said, what a life. More plates, Sam, and let's have a kiss.

40

Marc's apartment when he wasn't there seemed empty and abandoned. Walt, having swigged a long swallow of milk from the carton in the refrigerator, peed, sniffed the shaving brush, and made a face in the bathroom mirror, looked out all the windows.

Cyril, having drunk from the milk carton after Walt, peed, and looked out all the windows with Walt, fitted his chin onto Walt's shoulder.

—Sonia Terk, a Ukrainian, she was before she married Delaunay here in Paris. Grew up in St. Petersburg, which Maman says we're going to sometime. One of those Russian geniuses before the First World War. Sam liked it that you kissed him when we split at the metro. His dentist thinks she's Sam. If in Lapland a bear comes to eat you in the forest and you're a girl you pull down your britches and the bear blushes and goes away. You really do look like Kojève, except for the glasses. Let me look through 'em.

—Sam's the neatest friend in the whole world, isn't he? That tickles.

—Everything's a blur. Just flicking my tongue around your ear. Can you see without your specs?

—Sort of. If I do everything you do, will that be all right?

—And anything else, Maman's reading, and underlining in, a book by a Dutchman, Johan Huizinga, *Homo Ludens,* about games and sports. Does this tickle?

Cyril mirrored Walt's play of hands under his jersey, nubbling noses, rubbing insteps down the back of legs.

—Why is your mother writing about games?

—She's writing about Robert Delaunay's *The Cardiff Team,* and has to know all kinds of things, the life of Calixte Delmas and Baron Coubertin and the history of Ferris wheels and airplanes and clothes and whichwhat. We've got like an hour, maybe better. I think I understood Marc when we did the eye code.

41

While Walt banged tragic chords on the piano, Sam trotted in a dance of saucily tossed heels, singing with a sulky frown:

Nobody loves me
Everybody hates me
Going to the garden
To eat worms

Christofer, who had just arrived with Daisy, six feet six, ski sweater taxed by the beam of his shoulders, a flange of white hair over one eye, American jeans with canted fly, stood confused.

Walt attacked a dance from *Petrouschka* and Sam did Nijinski's puppet wobble.

—Hello Sam, hello Walt, Daisy said, boogying in with the Nijinski.

—Explain please, Christofer begged, staring at posters and prints on all the walls.

—It's just Walt and Sam full of themselves. At least they have on clothes, they usually don't.

—Peace! Penny shouted. Daisy and Christofer, you're here.

A kiss from Daisy, an enormous hand to shake from Christofer.

—Walter, as of this second you and Sam are waiters bringing in coffee when you've made it.

—Can we wear aprons?

—No.

A DAY IN THE COUNTRY

Cyril's hair a tuft of light, the morning sun caught in it through the train window, Walt sticking his fingers in it for the fun of mussing it, Marc reading *Le Parisien* left on a seat across the aisle, they wore their happiness, Walt, in Sam's curtailed denim pants, with grins and scheming eyes, Cyril, in Walt's, with dense patience and jiggling knee, Marc warily.

The day was still early when they fitted each other with their knapsacks at the country station and set out along the narrow road.

—I won't feel left out, Marc said, but who knows? Unless you've revised it again, Walt being inventive in these matters, you two as soon as we get there are going to dispense with the wearing of pants, together with all modesty and restraint?

—Well yes, Walt said. We've got all morning and all afternoon. Penny and Sam come out on the 7:10, and there's a train for Cyril back right after, if he can still walk and see straight. That's the best he could do with the jail he lives in.

—Neater than not getting to come at all. Cyril said. I'm being brave, you'll see. Walt says being shy is silly. But this isn't really happening.

—I did try, Marc said, to get you the day out here all by yourselves, in wild freedom, but Madame Secretary was having none of it. This is a nature outing, you understand, with me as scoutmaster, and Sam and Penny are along too, right now, a technical fib that the Recording Angel won't bother about. Upstairs will be all yours, for privacy. I've got weeding to do out back of the orchard, housecleaning, reading, a nap in the sun, and maybe an errand into the village.

—Stuff privacy, Walt said.

Cyril had never been in a small farmhouse, nor so rustic a garden, nor in the bottom of so much quiet.

—It started on the road. Our voices sound different. Listen. The silence is solid like, isn't it? Do you have fires in this fireplace?

—What I like is the smell, Walt said. Woodsmoke's part of it, cooking I suppose, mouse droppings probably, soap, wine. Country air, inside and out, has its own smell.

—Sitting by the fire, Marc said, with only its light, is part of the loveliness of this old house.

—It's even more storybook upstairs, Walt said. Off your pants, Cyril friend. I am.
—Let's sniff around more. The garden and orchard. The trees are old, old.
—Deckchairs in the shed around to the right. Get one and put it out for Marc at the end of the brick walk, where he likes to be. I hear him changing upstairs. We can be outside bare-ass.
—I see a rabbit!
—I'll show you cows and horses and sheep.
—I see that we aren't losing any time going savage, Marc said, coming downstairs in a ratty sweatshirt and frayed gym shorts, both with frazzled seams. I thought you're to do that with Cyril.
—Foreplay. He's talking to a rabbit.
—Cross-eyed, and with your tongue poked out.
—It feels that good, so quick. Thinking about it all the way out has made him seriously frisky. Cyril may hide under the bed, for all I know.
—Sex in the morning, Marc said, is always a little special.
—Anytime. Cyril, you dope!
—I want to see, Cyril said at the door, if I can take off my pants, and briefs too, here, with Marc watching and all. I think I'm going to be bashful, in spite of everything.
—We don't have to nip upstairs straightway just because I'm horny and up and full of loving kindness. Marc, tell Cyril some of the times you had at our age with your friends, in pup tents, in dormitories, in broad daylight.
—Cyril, Marc said, friends are friends. I'm as much a friend as Walt, and Walt's a very friendly fellow. Why don't both of you, charmingly britchesless, come help me get weeds out of the far end of the garden, in the warm sun, and get used to your freedom, and let things happen as they will.

Walt looked disappointed, Cyril pleased.
—OK, Walt said, but let's do the friendly kiss, on the corners of the mouth. Sam invented it, with its sexy tickle. Tribal greeting, Penny says.

—Marc, too?
—Absolutely, Marc said, kissing them both in passing.
—Neat! Walt said. Both corners for us, Cyril. Oh come on, hug.
—Get the wheelbarrow out of the shed, and find the trowel.
—Marc, Walt said, pulling his shirt over his head to be naked, tells inspiring tales of when he was a boy, crushes on friends he worshipped in locker rooms and at the swimming pool, and talked for hours with, and went everywhere with, but was too backward and bashful to jack off with, and wishes he had.
—Well, Marc said, not entirely. Put the wheelbarrow there. Let's see if we can find the borders of what I think are flower beds. Not all my friends were as bashful or as fastidious as I was.
—I'm taking everything off, Cyril said casually. What does fastidious mean?
—Being bashful about our bodies.
—Hugged and kissed all night with a friend he was giddy crazy about and was a champion masturbator, at least two or three times a day.
—Understand, Cyril, Marc said, that all this information was in answer to Walt's questions, as well as Sam's. Walt's curiosity, because of an upbringing of rather wide openness, deserves candor. At least, I think it does. You can't shock him with anything. You also understand that he's trying to get you upstairs and in bed, though he's not squeamish about playing Eros out here.
—What's squeamish?
—Same as fastidious.
—I like being naked out here. It feels good.
—A prominent and conspicuous part of Walt feels good too, Marc said.
—And better and better. You're looking adorable, Cyril. Come on, upstairs, huh?

43

Marc was coming upstairs.
—Walt! Toss me my sunglasses, can you? I don't dare come up. They're in my rucksack.
—Come get 'em yourself. Cyril has lost his mind and is a moron.
—No. Bad manners. I'll reach around the door.

Walt in a nimble jump friggled around in Marc's rucksack on the floor, sticking his head in for a comprehensive sniff, finding the glasses in a side pocket.
—I'm making some coffee for mid-morning break, if anybody's interested, or has deep idiocy set in beyond the reach of the phenomenal world?

Silence.

Backing down the stairs, Marc heard *adding some spit for slick* and Cyril's *nobody's objecting.*
—Hey! Sure, we'll be down in a while.
—I'm out having a sunbath. Coffee's dripping through. Get your own and bring it out, if you can walk straight.

44

At the end of the brick walk, the big pear tree behind him, Marc in a deck chair taking the bright summer sun had finished his coffee before Cyril and Walt joined him.
—You're about to ask us, Walt said, if we're in our right minds. We are, and Cyril's much smarter than when we went upstairs, you won't believe how much. You need more coffee.
—I'll get it, Cyril said.

An exchange of smiles, Marc lifting his sunglasses so that his eyes could be seen.
—Time quits when you're having fun.
—Walt, what are you doing, exactly?

—Sniffing your underwears.
—We're friends.

Cyril, returning with Marc's coffee, stopped in midstep, mouth open, one foot still raised.

—What's Walt doing?
—Inhaling the odor of my briefs, presumably delectable.
—Holy blue. But who's surprised? I got sniffed all over. I feel like somebody else.
—You probably are somebody else, Marc said. Walt does that to people. In a bit we're going down to the village to get lunch, but not just yet.
—It's not bright to sniff people, is it?
—No, but it's natural.
—Beautiful.
—Now what are you doing?
—Taking off your underwears, so you'll be as Greek as us, and get brown all over, and Cyril can stare. Lift your behind. Golly.
—This is a lovely place, Cyril said. The orchard.
—Osmesis, Marc said. Fancy word for sniffing. The locals, in passing, have learned that if you peep through the hedge you see wildly interesting things. A few weekends back a blue-eyed little boy with two hundred freckles got to see Walt measuring his dick with a ruler, debating with me whether the length along the top, the sides, or the keel was the true extent.

Cyril laughed with half his attention, as he was trying to look without seeming to at Marc's nudity, half risen.

—In the newspaper, Walt said, it told about some Swedish teenagers at summer Bible camp up in the high meadows in the north who smeared marmalade all over each other and licked it off. One of them was the crown prince, who's fifteen. His mama, the queen, said the beauty of the scenery excited them. That's what she told the newspaper. You shook hands with my dink when I gave you your sunglasses.
—To be friendly.

—It was. Cyril's ticklish in odd places. Where do you suppose they smeared the marmalade, everywhere?

45

The restaurant in the village had served them cold chicken with mayonnaise, heaps of fried potatoes, a spinach salad with crusts, and chocolate cake with whipped cream. They'd sat at a long trestle table under a tree. They shared the table with a stout local citizen of two chins and hair combed sideways across a bald pate, a middle-aged woman in a flowery dress who smiled at them and guessed that they were Parisians, and a large dog who accepted scraps and bones from them all, which it swallowed with an eager snap and without any formality of chewing.

—Exemplary, Marc replied to Walt's asking if they had been civilized enough. Kissing the dog on the nose was perhaps not in the best of taste, but all in all I'm proud of you. Only the solid citizen saw you squeezing each other's crotches.

—But we didn't, Cyril said. Did we, Walt?

—Sort of thing I assumed you were doing, Marc said. What were you doing, then, that elicited disapproval from one of his eyes and fascination from the other?

—Well, it may have been when you were talking to the dog and Walt passed cake from his mouth to mine.

—We rubbed knees some.

—Cyril will soon be a rascal. Not yet, quite, but making good progress.

—Were you a rascal, Marc? Cyril asked.

—No, but Walt and Sam think I should make up for it. I'm doing a little better, would you say, Walt?

Walt grinned.

—You see? Marc said. Nothing's enough for the little twit. I take on the job, willingly and happily, of being his big brother, at great risk to my sanity, and what do I get but a silly grin? Shall we show Cyril more pigs and cows and fields of sunflowers, or go straight back?

—Both, Walt said. I'll bet Cyril has never waded in a creek. If we get in the creek up ahead, we can walk along it and get to the field that's in back of our orchard.

—Are you making this up?

—Sam and I have done it. Met two cows standing in the creek and petted them. It's not over knee-deep anywhere, and has silver sardines in it, and bugs that walk backwards on the water.

—Sold, Marc said. We tie our shoelaces together, right, and hang our shoes around our neck.

Rippled light played on their legs as they waded in, Marc's jeans rolled to his knees. Dragonflies shuttling, butterflies drinking sunshine through their wings, nebulae of gnats.

—The wettest of smells, Walt said, a country creek.

A lizard on a rock, leaving.

—It changes the sound of our voices, Cyril said, but in a way different from the road and the orchard.

—And how, Walt said, trying to close cupped hands around a butterfly, can I take my pants off over wet feet?

—I'm not asking, Marc said, why you must take off your pants.

—To be naked.

—Watch, Cyril said. One leg at a time, with hands inside, like so, and one wet foot comes through, just. Then the other.

—Cyril's a genius. Here, roll our shirts and pants together.

Marc waded into a pool at a bend, stooping to look under an overhang of bramble and haw.

—Cyril, he said, do you know that you haven't had your glasses on all morning, not since you and Walt, panting with lust, galloped up to the bed?

Cyril stood with a wondering stare.

—So I haven't!

—Can you see? Walt asked. I hadn't mentioned it, to find out how long it would take you to notice.

—Monet would have liked these poplars, Marc said, unzipping his jeans to pee against the bank.
—A friendly pee, Walt said. Come on, Cyril.
—Not in the creek, the minnows' world and home.
—If we had dicks like Marc's, Walt said, the bedroom ceiling would be one stupendous mess. If you'd worn your bottom-of-the-laundry-bag gym pants, you could be like us.
—We have an open field to traverse to get to the house, and the locals would neglect the cows and the poultry talking about it. They're probably right now calling each other to report on our progress upstream, two of them mother-naked, one of them playing with himself.
—Both of them, Cyril said. How could anybody see us, and anyway, I'm not going to be bashful ever again. That goes for kicking water on people, too.

Marc, turning to Walt with a frowning smile, heaved him up and set him on his shoulders, facing backwards.
—Have a look around.
—Five cows, several families of grackles, the church steeple, a blond horse, and my tummy is being kissed.
—No locals?
—Not unless they're around the bend up the creek, where all you can see is shrubbery. Let Cyril look, too. You've not tasted him yet, and with his glasses off he can probably see through things.

Walt monkeyed down, jumped and splashed. Cyril splashed back, put his foot in Marc's hands, climbed, and straddled his shoulders.
—Swivel around the other way, Marc said, and get snuggled like Walt. Eros is the most inventive of the gods, with an IQ way out beyond Einstein's.

Cyril obeyed, while saying that he wouldn't swear to the number of cows, would call the horse white, and didn't see any grackles at all. He bent over and hugged Marc's neck.

—Slide around piggyback, Marc said, and I'll give you a ride back to the house. If we get out of the creek here, and go on a diagonal uphill, won't that do it?

Walt scouted ahead, bouncing.

—Fish the keys, Walt, out of my pocket and nip through the house and let us in the orchard gate, and put on your pants.

—Mna, Walt said, skittering away.

46

Penny, floppy cardigan and jeans, laying out supper from a charcuterie, said that she'd never seen a little boy who wanted more to cry and yet was wildly happy.

—He got on the train as if he were a young Russian intellectual off to Siberia.

—I'll need Walt's help to tell it all, Marc said, uncorking the wine. Cyril is either shooting his father and the housekeeper and the chauffeur in the crime of the century, or has thrown himself into the traffic on the Etoile. We'll walk down to the village after supper and call to see that he got home.

—You had lunch in the village, outside, and waded in the creek, I gather, and Cyril saw a rabbit and a pig that took his fancy, and had a lovely day of it. I long ago gave up trying to decode Walt and Sam's Choctaw.

—As the day went on, Cyril got over being shy in a large way and began to be a replica, but not quite, of Walt. Shyness, however, has its charm, and must have its evolutionary uses.

—Of course it has.

—You should have seen the orchard about two hours ago. They came down from the bedroom and got me. I was innocently reading in the deckchair here. You're dead right about curiosity.

SANTAYANA

It is pleasant to think that the fertility of spirit is inexhaustible, if matter only gives it a chance, and that the worst and most successful fanaticism cannot turn the moral world into a desert.

48

September, the long meadow that slopes from the orchard down to the stream. The grass, still green, was speckled with archipelagoes of late summer flowers. The day was warm.
—Rimbaud, yes, Marc said to Cyril. *The summer dawn wakes up the leaves.* Not everybody reads Rimbaud with breakfast.
—*Over there,* Cyril recited, *to your right, a summer dawn wakes up the leaves. The mists, the rustle in this corner of the park, while the slant to your left keeps the thousand wheelruts in the mud of the road in violet shadow.* Why a thousand? Big number, I suppose, and roads, like meadows, are one of Rimbaud's things.
—He counts the wagons, too: twenty, and the horses.
—Circus wagons full of children and merry-go-round animals, made of wood, painted bright colors, and gilded.
—*And the horses' black plumes nod.*
—Pastoral with gypsies, circus wagons going from country fair to country fair. A procession of children in carnival costumes.
—A pageant. And, as he says, the wagons are like something in a folktale. Walt can explain it, and Bee will explain it exactly the opposite, for the fun of it.
—Bee? not Sam?
—Sam would agree with Walt, loyally. If, of course, anybody can claim to know what Sam or Walt is going to say. Walt can quote Rimbaud beautifully, at unexpected times. Once, at my place, I was wondering how anybody so recently delivered by the stork as Walt could look out the side of his lovely eyes, albeit slitted with mischief, like the sultan's favorite houri, while,

moreover, swigging milk from the carton. I said so, and he came back with *the paths are uneven, the knolls thick with sedge, the air still, no springs or birds anywhere near, and, up ahead, the end of the world.* He was wanting to be nasty, only hours after I'd seen him and Bee licking each other, at Penny's, where I was for our afternoon fuck. Later, going to pee, it was impossible not to see them, Belgian buck hare and doe, their door wide open of course.

—Of course.

—Penny was accusing me of being a billy goat, as she thought we were at the snuggle-and-catnap afterwards part, and, if we're talking as I think we are, I was inspired all over again, and was shoving in when here was Walt in the bedroom saying *awesome! Henri Pélissier, yellow jersey, 1924. Marc's checking out bike designs and physiques.*

—And when I was sent to your seminar I thought I was in for the dullest hours I'd ever have to suffer. I'm somebody else now, you know?

—You were somebody else then. You're yourself now, or beginning to be. Walt and Sam liked you from the start, but they weren't quite certain what to make of you.

—They scared me pissless.

—Daisy has finished the big canvas and sent it off to Amsterdam. I've got a working draft of my poem, in which I hope there's a lot of this meadow, and the orchard, and you and Sam and Walt. Penny's work on *The Cardiff Team* is going to be a whole issue of *Les Cahiers d'Art*. If Walt were here, he'd say *I see a lion already.* What would Sam reply?

—Lion, lion. *From the Hambourg Zoo.* That's what she'd say, from Apollinaire. *Blue eyes.*

—You've mastered their style. You call Sam *she* now?

—She asked me to. She's going to let her hair grow, and wear dresses. I think Walt's grieving.

—This lion, did the sons of heaven come down to shred gold for its mane?

—Is that a poem?
—A Welsh one, very old. Penny's Delaunay's footballers would have learned it in school, though it's of a girl's hair, not a lion's mane.

Footballers, smelling of oranges.

—Do you remember our ramble in the forest at Saint-Germain, where we found a clearing along a gamekeeper's path?

A brocade moth asleep on licorice.

—A meadow in the middle of the forest, oh yes. One of the times Walt and Sam befuddled me grandly with their talk of smooching in the Parc Vincennes, kissing for an hour in a field of sunbathers, seeing, as they bragged, how long they could tickle tongues before slipping warm hands into each other's pants. I think you saw what such talk *did* to me, because you teased them, until they admitted that they'd groped each other until they were gibbering, then fed each other Swiss chocolate and orange slices, like mama birds. I realize how kindly you protected me from their trying to shock me.

—The stork-loading assembly line certainly wasn't stingy when they fitted Walt out for making babies. Some naughty angel thought an outsized generator was just the thing to go with his good looks. Walt says he inherited it from the sailor whose name his mother forgot to ask.

—Both that sailor and my father have sons they don't know.

—I wonder if we can believe in that sailor?

—My father is not to be believed. Nor my mother. We can add her.

—Montherlant says in *Les Olympiques* that Polycrates burnt the gymnasiums of Samos because he knew that every friendship forged in them was two revolutionaries. Our real families are our friends, who of course may be family as well. Walt and Sam have not yet found the country they want to be citizens of. You and I, Cyril, are immigrants in the imaginary country Penny and Daisy founded, with a population of four.

—Bee's getting pubic hair, which she's proud of, and breasts,

which are beautiful. She's out of Maillol's *Georgics.* I think I'm walking around in a dream.
—No, only in a poem. Or a Balthus painting. There are forty-two wars raging right now, never mind the private unhappinesses everywhere, pain, disease, and hatred. We are here in this meadow. Even it has no reality we can know other than how our imagination perceives it.

Que parfois la Nature, à notre réveil, nous propose
Ce à quoi justement nous étions disposés,
La louange aussitôt s'enfle dans notre gorge.
Nous croyons être au paradis.

Our sense of the beautiful is illusory, a cooperation of culture and biological imperative. We have senses that must be educated into sensitivities or be blunted into stupidity. You have become beautiful by letting your hair grow, though it needs another month, and because you look like an elf, and because you smile now and speak your mind.
—Was I so awful?
—Of course not. *Une espèce de microbe* you weren't, and can never have been.
—And have thrown my glasses away. And I think I've proved at the gym with you that I don't have a rheumatic heart or asthma or any of the things they've used to scare me with. Penny says you are so beautiful she blushes, still, every time you come into a room. Is it all right to say that? I think so, too.
Marc halted. They had walked the length of the meadow, then across it, and were in the middle of it.
—They've harvested the field of sunflowers across the stream, that was all gold and green, Cyril said. Remember our wonderful wading up the stream two months back, was it?
Marc sat, looking up at Cyril.
—You're not feeling left out?
—Oh no.
—The great thing, Marc said, is taking things in. Penny says that

kindly angels might lead her through a study of Braque. I love her for that, love that in her. They've discovered that there are stars older than the universe. So much to learn, so much to take in. I've been reading an English writer of the last century, name of Landor, and found a passage about a young Greek of the fifth century, Hegemon, age fifteen, whose curls are pressed down by the famous *saloniste* Aspasia, with her finger, to see them spring up again. He bit her finger for the liberty she had taken, and said he must kiss it to make it well, and perhaps kiss her elsewhere, here and there, to prevent the spreading of the venom. Playing Eros, he was.

Cyril sat in front of Marc, toe to toe.

—Greeks, he said. Their friendships in the gymnasiums that could overthrow tyrants. That scares me, a bit, still.

Midges.

—It scared me, surprised me is more like it, when I saw how much I liked the hitch of Sam's and Walt's britches, and how fascinated I was by Walt's doggy sniffing. And licking and feeling.

—Yes. Oh God, yes.

—We're metamorphic beings, like tadpoles and frogs. Walt has a savage's curiosity and Penny's sophistication, so that he's crazy and sane all at once. You know him better than I.

—No I don't. He counts on not having to explain things to you. He says that when he wanted to see your dick erect, you obliged without making a do about it.

—He also wanted to know why everything on my desk was arranged as it was, and what some books on my shelves were about, and to see my socks, shirts, trousers, and briefs, raincoat and jackets. He asked about all the prints on the walls. He asked questions as tactless as a doctor's and as pointless as a psychiatrist's. All this was reported to Sam, who went into it more thoroughly.

—Why did this one old pear tree get left here in the middle of the meadow?

—To sit under at noon, maybe, or for cows to stand in its shade. It may have marked a boundary.
—What about they couldn't bear to cut it down? They liked its pears.
—And blossoms in the spring. Its presence throughout the year.

> But there's a Tree, of many, one,
> A single Field which I have locked upon.
> Both of them speak of something that is gone.

—Is that Shakespeare? It's warm enough for us to be Vergilian, wouldn't you say?
—Wordsworth. You're wearing a FREE NEW CALEDONIA button.
—Walt gave it to me. In the Pacific, isn't it, an old French colony, people by Gauguin exploited by cartels?
—Not barefoot terrain, this, but if you think we should be barefoot, barefoot we'll be.
—And shirtless. For the last of the summer.
—It is a fine day, yes, August still. Fold everything into squares stacked on your shoes, or the ants, who are going to eat us, will colonize our clothes. We should have brought a blanket.
—Not Vergilian, a blanket. They're not coming back until tomorrow, right? And Daisy's in Amsterdam. We can be Vergilian here at the edge of the shade, and look up into the branches. Tell me what Wordsworth meant and about your poem.
—Wordsworth meant that what we see is always memory. *The Field Path* my poem's called. It is, I suppose, a longish meditation. It doesn't have the weave of Ponge's "Le Pré," I'm not that good. It's a kind of photograph by Bernard Faucon. Walt and Sam once brought me a notebook in which they said they were writing down *things of awesome importance.* This turned out to be their jotting about places, England and Denmark, with some astute observations on learning a new place. Experiences: snuggled under the covers here listening to rain, the stamp market at the Rond Point, lots of things they say I said and which I scarcely

recognized. Outings with Penny, with Daisy, with me. Of this meadow I remember a passage about midges sawing and spiralling because there was no wind, and would a wind carry them kilometres away? *The Big Wheel is the Eiffel Tower's American wife.* So I began a notebook of my own, and have been making the poem out of what I've put into it.
—I'll get a notebook. Put this afternoon in it. Do we take off everything?
—No *slips Hom micro* in Vergil, not even ones as obliquely angled out as yours.
—It's nature, as Walt says.
—A blushing grin may be one of nature's best acts. Up there with bears having their lunch in the Jardin d'Acclimatation, Penny soaping up Bee in her bath, and Walt crossing his eyes and jutting his tongue when he slides his foreskin back on the first pull. Walt's genius is that he would have been thinking about it for hours before, in and out of the other concerns of the world, Walt's world, which only sometimes coincides with the one called real.
—That's how it is with me too, anymore. Like Walt, and like the neat kid on the Dutch poster in Walt and Sam's room, wearing nothing but a smile, that says he's the boss of inside his underpants.
—*Baas in eigen broekje.* Daisy got that in Amsterdam.
—To see like you and Penny, to learn things, to talk, to come and go when I want to. I've been collecting ambitions all summer.
—One of the things I learned at your age was that finding out about what's in books and the world and feeling great in my pants were cooperative. I thought it was just me, the way I was. Mind and body are alive together. And here we are with the ants, midges, and ground spiders.
—Grasshoppers and butterflies.
—The sun is delicious. A warmth with kindness in it.
—I like this. It's now and it's books and paintings. Say that Greek poem about how they were aware of themselves.

In naked Spartan light
Old men sang
We were a handsome sight
When we were young.

Little boys beside them sang
So shall we be,
And braver in the long
Run. Wait and see.

The young men sang
What these were,
What these shall be,
We now are.

—I would have been one of the littles, scared but perky.
—In a skimpy Spartan shirt inherited from an older brother, or in nothing, knees and elbows rusty, a true believer in geometry, Eros, and the alphabet. Rocking a loose milk tooth with your tongue.
—The sky through the leaves is both green and blue. New Caledonia, the button Walt gave me, tell me about it. That's my ear you're playing with and I'm not jumping out of my skin.
—There was a Pastor Leenhardt, Maurice Leenhardt, a Huguenot, son of a Calvinist geologist.
—Huguenot, Calvinist. Our voices in the middle of a field are not our voices in rooms, or even in the orchard.
—He and his wife Jeanne went to New Caledonia in the early part of the century, as missionaries. He liked to say, later, when he was an ethnologist lecturing at the Sorbonne (he held the chair Lévi-Strauss took over when he retired), that he did not convert a single Canaque but that he was converted by them.
—I like that. His conversion, I mean.
—He changed Lévy-Bruhl's ideas about the savage mind. They were great friends, and had long walks in the Bois practically

every afternoon, two wonderful old men who recognized each other's humanity.
—Lovely.
—Swivel around, so that I can get at more of you, and close up ranks against the ants. He discovered that the New Caledonians had a religion perhaps superior in many ways to what he had come to teach them, and harmonized his theology with theirs. They loved him, but were more interested in learning to sew with French needles and thread, and to cook in our pots and pans, but what they liked most was arithmetic, for the magic poetry of it, and so that European merchants couldn't cheat them. They made hymns of the multiplication table which they sang in church.
—That's wonderful, isn't it? Cyril said.

Five times five be twenty-five,
Five times six be thirty!
Five times seven be thirty-five,
Five times eight be forty!

Five times nine be forty-five,
Five times ten be fifty!
Five times eleven be fifty-five,
Five times twelve be sixty!

NOTES AND ACKNOWLEDGMENTS

THE MESSENGERS

This fourth of my stories about Kafka (the others are "The Aeroplanes at Brescia" in *Tatlin!*, "The Chair" in *Apples and Pears*, and "Belinda's World Tour" in *A Table of Green Fields*) derives from his diary for 1912.

DINNER AT THE BANK OF ENGLAND

The occasion is recorded in George Santayana's autobiography *Persons and Places*. The identity of the captain of the guards is given in the notes to William G. Holzberger and Herman J. Saatkamp Jr.'s critical edition, M.I.T. Press, 1986. The passage at the end about the old man with a guitar—the instigation (not Picasso's painting) for Wallace Stevens's "The Man with the Blue Guitar"—is from Santayana's *The Realms of Being*.

BOYS SMELL LIKE ORANGES

The two old men walking in the Bois are Maurice Leenhardt (1878–1954), missionary and ethnologist, and Lucien Lévy-Bruhl (1857–1938). I am indebted to Rodney Needham's *Belief, Language, and Experience* (1972) and James Clifford's *Person and Myth: Maurice Leenhardt in the Melanesian World* (1982), as well as to Leenhardt's *Do kamo* (1947) and Lévy-Bruhl's *Carnets posthumes* (1949). The passages about soccer players are freely adapted from a few pages of Henry de Montherlant's classic *Les Olympiques*, a Theokritean idyll which I have lifted out and collaged into my text, sometimes translating *ad verbum*, always performing variations (in the musical sense): Peyrony does not eat quite so much grass and leaves in Montherlant.

THE MEADOW LARK

Section III quotes Balzac.

VERANDA HUNG WITH WISTERIA

Poe's *Eureka* is dedicated to Alexander von Humboldt (1769–1859). His *Cosmos: A Physical Description of the Universe* (4 vols.) began to be published in English in 1845.

THE CARDIFF TEAM

The opening paragraph quotes Francis Ponge's "Le Pré."

The book being read at bedtime in Section 9 is Sigismund Krzyzanowski's *Vospominaniya O Budushchem* (Moscow 1989) in the French translation of Catherine Perrel and Elena Rolland-Maiski (1991).

Section 13 is from *Scientific American,* 18 May 1889.

Section 18 is from *Scientific American,* 1 July 1893.

Section 31 translates Henry de Montherlant's *"Sur des souliers de foot"* (in *Les Olympiques*).

Section 38 translates Vicente Huidobro's *"Pour Robert Delaunay."*